Nora Roberts

Two of a Kind

🔻™ *Silhouette* Books

Published by Silhouette Books

America's Publisher of Contemporary Romance

SILHOUETTE BOOKS

TWO OF A KIND

ISBN 0-373-28515-9

Copyright © 2005 by Harlequin Books S.A.

The publisher acknowledges the copyright holders
of the individual works as follows:

IMPULSE
Copyright: © 1989 by Nora Roberts

THE BEST MISTAKE
Copyright: © 1994 by Nora Roberts

CONTENTS

Dear Reader,

Silhouette Books is proud to bring readers this extraspecial gift hardcover, *Two of a Kind,* containing two of Nora Roberts's novellas about summer romance—and how to keep that love, not just for a season but for all time.

The English playwright Christopher Marlowe once wrote, "Who ever loved that loved not at first sight?" In "Impulse," Rebecca Malone finds her very own head-over-heels love when she leaves behind her mundane life in Philadelphia and heads for the sun-drenched islands of Greece. There she meets the sophisticated, sexy Stephen Nickodemus, who romances her in sizzling sunlight and Mediterranean moonlight. Can their summer love endure the season's end?

Bachelor journalist Cooper MacKinnon isn't the type to take on a ready-made family, but Coop is captivated by single mom Zoe Fleming and her young son. Zoe's been burned too many times to rely on poetry and flowers, and empty promises. But as Shakespeare once wrote, "Love looks not with the eyes, but with the mind." Is love truly "The Best Mistake" of all?

Fun fact: Did you know that Nora Roberts wrote five novellas for Silhouette Books? Besides these two, there are two Christmas tales, and a historical MacGregor story that introduces us to an ancestor of the famous MacGregor family.

Enjoy!

The Editors

IMPULSE

CHAPTER 1

She knew it was crazy. That was what she liked best about it. It was crazy, ridiculous, impractical and totally out of character. And she was having the time of her life. From the balcony of her hotel suite Rebecca could see the sweep of the beach, the glorious blue of the Ionian Sea, blushed now with streaks of rose from the setting sun.

Corfu. Even the name sounded mysterious, exciting, glamorous. And she was here, really here. Practical, steady-as-a-rock Rebecca Malone, who had never traveled more than five hundred miles from Philadelphia, was in Greece. Not just in Greece, she thought with a grin, but on the exotic island of Corfu, in one of the most exclusive resorts in Europe.

First-class, she thought as she leaned out to let the

sweet breeze ruffle over her face. As long as it lasted, she was going first-class.

Her boss had thought she was suffering from temporary insanity. Edwin McDowell of McDowell, Jableki and Kline was never going to understand why a promising young CPA would resign from her position with one of the top accounting firms in Philadelphia. She'd made a good salary, she'd enjoyed excellent benefits, and she'd even had a small window in her office.

Friends and associates had wondered if she'd suffered a breakdown. After all, it wasn't normal, and it certainly wasn't Rebecca's style to quit a solid, well-paying job without the promise of a better one.

But she'd given her two weeks' notice, cleared out her desk and had cheerfully walked out into the world of the unemployed.

When she'd sold her condo and then in one frantic week, auctioned off every possession she owned— every stick of furniture, every pot and pan and appliance—they'd been certain she'd gone over the edge.

Rebecca had never felt saner.

She owned nothing that didn't fit in a suitcase. She no longer had any tax-deferred investments or retirement plans. She'd cashed in her certificates of deposit, and the home entertainment center she'd thought she couldn't live without was now gracing someone else's home.

It had been more than six weeks since she'd even looked at a calculator.

For the first—and perhaps the only—time in her life, she was totally free. There were no responsibilities, no pressures, no hurried gulps of cold coffee. She hadn't packed an alarm clock. She no longer owned one. Crazy? No. Rebecca shook her head and laughed into the breeze. For as long as it lasted, she was going to grab life with both hands and see what it had to offer.

Aunt Jeannie's death had been her turning point. It had come so suddenly, so unexpectedly, leaving Rebecca without any family. Aunt Jeannie had worked hard for most of her sixty-five years, always punctual, always responsible. Her position as head librarian had been her whole life. She'd never missed a day, never failed to do her duty. Her bills had been paid on time. Her promises had always been kept.

More than once Rebecca had been told she took after her mother's older sister. She was twenty-four, but she was—had been—as solid and sturdy as her maiden aunt. Two months into retirement, two months after dear Aunt Jeannie began to make plans to travel, to enjoy the rewards she'd worked so hard to earn, she was gone.

After Rebecca's grief had come the anger, then the frustration, then slowly, the realization that she was traveling the same straight road. She worked, she slept, she fixed well-balanced meals that she ate alone. She had a small circle of friends who knew she could be counted on in a crisis. Rebecca would always find the best and most practical answer. Rebecca would never drop her own problems in your lap—because she didn't have any. Rebecca, bless her, was a port in any storm.

She hated it, and she'd begun to hate herself. She had to do something.

And she was doing it.

It wasn't running away as much as it was breaking free. All her life she'd done what was expected of her and tried to make as few waves as possible while doing it. All through school a crushing shyness had kept her more comfortable with her books than with other teenagers. In college a need to succeed and justify her aunt's faith had locked her tightly into her studies.

She had always been good with figures—logical, thorough, patient. It had been easy, perhaps too easy, to pour herself into that one area, because there, and really only there, had she felt confident.

Now she was going to discover Rebecca Malone. In the weeks or months of freedom she had, she wanted to learn everything there was to know about the woman within. Perhaps there wasn't a butterfly inside the cocoon she'd wrapped herself in so comfortably, but whatever she found—whoever she found—Rebecca hoped she would enjoy her, like her, perhaps even respect her.

When the money ran out, she'd get another job and go back to being plain, practical Rebecca. Until that time she was rich, rootless and ready for surprises.

She was also hungry.

Stephen saw her the moment she entered the restaurant. It wasn't that she was particularly striking. Beautiful women passed through the world every day and they usually warranted a glance. But there was something about the way this one walked, as if she were ready for anything, even looking forward to it. He stopped, and because business was slow at this hour he took a second, longer look.

She was tall for a woman, and more angular than slender. Her skin was pale, and that made him think she had only just arrived at the resort or was shy of the sun. The white sundress that left her shoulders and back bare accented the lack of color and gave dramatic contrast to her short cap of raven hair.

She paused, then seemed to take a deep breath. Stephen could almost hear her satisfied sigh. Then she smiled at the headwaiter, and followed him to her table, tossing her head back, so that her hair, which she wore arrow-straight, swung away from her chin.

A nice face, Stephen concluded. Bright, intelligent,

eager. Especially the eyes. They were pale, an almost translucent gray. But there was nothing pale in their expression. She smiled at the waiter again, then laughed and looked around the restaurant. She looked as if she'd never been happier in her life.

She saw him. When Rebecca's gaze first skimmed over the man leaning against the bar, her automatic shyness kicked in and had her looking away. Attractive men had stared at her before—though it wasn't exactly a daily event. She'd never been able to handle it with the aplomb—or even cynicism—of most of her contemporaries. To cover her momentary embarrassment, she lifted her menu.

He hadn't meant to linger more than a few moments longer, but the impulse came suddenly. Stephen flicked a hand at the waiter and had him scurrying over, nodding quickly at Stephen's murmured request and hurrying off. When he returned it was to deliver a bottle of champagne to Rebecca's table.

"Compliments of Mr. Nickodemus."

"Oh." Rebecca followed the waiter's gaze over to the man by the bar. "Well, I—" She brought herself up short before she could stammer. A sophisticated woman wouldn't stutter over a gift of champagne, she reminded herself. She'd accept it graciously, with dignity. And maybe—if she wasn't a complete fool—she'd relax enough to flirt with the man who offered it.

Stephen watched the expressions pass across her face. Fascinating, he mused, and realized that the vague boredom he'd been feeling had vanished. When she lifted her head and smiled at him, he had no idea that her heart was pounding. He saw only a casual invitation, and he answered it.

He wasn't just attractive, Rebecca realized as he crossed to her table. He was gorgeous. Eye-popping, mouth-dropping gorgeous. She had an image of Apollo and ancient Greek warriors. Thick blond hair streaked by the sun fell over the collar of his shirt. Smooth, bronzed skin was marred—and somehow enhanced— by a faint scar under his jawline. A strong jaw, she thought. A strong face, with the darkest, deepest blue eyes she'd ever seen.

"Good evening, I'm Stephen Nickodemus." His voice wasn't accented, it was rounded, rich. He might have come from anywhere. Perhaps it was that, more than anything else, that intrigued her.

Lecturing herself on poise and image, she lifted her hand. "Hello. I'm Rebecca, Rebecca Malone." She felt a quick flutter when he brushed his lips over her knuckles. Feeling foolish, she drew her hand away and balled it in her lap. "Thank you for the champagne."

"It seemed to suit your mood." He studied her, wondering why he was getting such a mix of signals. "You are by yourself?"

"Yes." Perhaps it was a mistake to admit it, but if she was going to live life to the fullest she had to take some risks. The restaurant wasn't crowded, but they were hardly alone. Take the plunge, she told herself, and tried another smile. "The least I can do is offer you a glass."

Stephen took the seat across from her, brushing the waiter aside to pour the wine himself. "You are American?"

"It shows."

"No. Actually, I thought you were French until you spoke."

"Did you?" That pleased her. "I've just come from Paris." She had to force herself not to touch her hair. She'd had it cut, with trepidation and delight, in a French salon.

Stephen touched his glass to hers. Her eyes bubbled with life as cheerfully as the wine. "Business?"

"No, just pleasure." What a marvelous word, she thought. *Pleasure.* "It's a wonderful city."

"Yes. Do you go often?"

Rebecca smiled into her glass. "Not often enough. Do you?"

"From time to time."

She nearly sighed at that. Imagine anyone speaking of going to Paris "from time to time." "I nearly stayed longer, but I'd promised myself Greece."

So she was alone, restless, and on the move. Perhaps

that was why she had appealed to him, because he was, too. "Is Corfu your first stop?"

"Yes." She sipped at her drink. A part of her still believed it was all a dream. Greece, champagne, the man. "It's beautiful. Much more beautiful than I imagined it could be."

"It's your first trip, then?" He couldn't have said why that pleased him. "How long do you stay?"

"As long as I like." She grinned, savoring the feeling of freedom. "And you?"

He lifted his glass. "Longer, I think, than I had planned." When the waiter appeared at his side, Stephen handed over the menu, then spoke to him in soft, quick Greek. "If you don't object, I'd like to guide you through your first meal on the island."

The old Rebecca would have been too nervous to sit through a meal with a stranger. The new Rebecca took a second, deeper sip of champagne. "I'd love it. Thank you."

It was easy. Easy to sit, to laugh, to sample new and exotic tastes. She forgot that he was a stranger, forgot that the world she was living in now was only temporary. They didn't speak of anything important—only of Paris, and the weather, and the wine. Still, she was sure it was the most interesting conversation of her life. He looked at her when he spoke to her, looked at her as though he were delighted to spend an hour talking of nothing. The last man she'd had dinner with had wanted her to give him a discount when she did his taxes.

Stephen wasn't asking her for anything more than her company for dinner. When he looked at her it seemed unlikely that he'd care if she knew how to fill out Schedule C.

When he suggested a walk along the beach, she agreed without a qualm. What better way to end an evening than a walk in the moonlight?

"I was looking out at this from my window just before dinner." Rebecca stepped out of her shoes, then dangled them from her fingers as she walked. "I didn't think it could look more beautiful than it did at sunset."

"The sea changes, like a woman, in the light." He paused to touch a flame to the end of a slim cigar. "So men are drawn to her."

"Are you? Drawn to the sea?"

"I've spent my time on her. I fished in these waters as a boy."

She'd learned at dinner that he'd grown up traveling the islands with his father. "It must have been exciting, moving from place to place, seeing new things almost every day."

He shrugged. He'd never been sure whether the restlessness had been born in him or had been a product of his upbringing. "It had its moments."

"I love to travel." Laughing, she tossed her shoes aside, then stepped into the surf. The champagne was making her head swim and the moonlight felt as soft as rain. "I adore it." She laughed again when the spray washed up to dampen her skirts. The Ionian Sea. She was standing in it. "On a night like this I think I'll never go home."

She looked so vibrant, so alive, standing in the surf with her white skirts billowing. "Where's home?"

She glanced over her shoulder. The flirtatious look was totally unplanned and completely devastating. "I haven't decided. I want to swim." On impulse, she dived into the surf.

Stephen's heart stopped when she disappeared. He'd already kicked off his shoes and started forward when she rose up again. For a second time, his heart stopped.

She was laughing, her face lifted to the moonlight. Water cascaded from her hair, from her skin. The drops that clung to her were the only jewels she wore. Beautiful? No, she wasn't beautiful. She was electric.

"It's wonderful. Cool and soft and wonderful."

With a shake of his head, he stepped in far enough to take her hand and pull her toward shore. She was a little mad, perhaps, but engagingly so. "Are you always so impulsive?"

"I'm working on it. Aren't you?" She combed her

hand through her dripping hair. "Or do you always send champagne to strange women?"

"Either way I answer that could be trouble. Here." He shrugged out of his jacket and draped it over her shoulders. Unframed, washed clean, her face glowed in the moonlight. There was a graceful kind of strength in it, to the sweep of cheekbone, the slightly pointed chin. Delicate—except for the eyes. One look there showed power, a power that was still. "You're irresistible, Rebecca."

She stared at him, confused all over again, as he gathered the neck of the jacket close around her throat. "I'm wet," she managed.

"And beautiful." With his hands still on the jacket, he brought her toward him. "And fascinating."

That made her laugh again. "I don't think so, but thanks. I'm glad you sent me the champagne and guided me through my first meal." Her nerves began to jangle. His eyes stayed on hers, journeying only once to her mouth, which was still damp from the sea. Their bodies were close, close enough to brush. Rebecca began to shiver, and she knew it had nothing to do with wet clothes and the breeze.

"I should go in…change my dress."

There was something about her. The impulsiveness, the easy flirtatiousness, hid an unmistakable innocence that baffled and attracted him. Whatever it was, he wanted more.

"I'll see you again."

"Yes." She prayed for her heartbeat to slow. "It's not a very big island."

He smiled at that, slowly. She felt, with a mixture of relief and regret, the relaxation of his hands. "Tomorrow. I have business early. I'll be done by eleven, if that suits you. I'll show you Corfu."

"All right." Better judgment and nerves be damned. She wanted to go with him. "I'll meet you in the lobby." Carefully, because she suddenly wasn't sure she could manage it, she stepped back. Moonlight silhouetted him against the sea. "Good night, Stephen."

She forgot to be sophisticated and dashed toward the hotel.

He watched her go. She puzzled him, puzzled him as no woman had since he'd been a boy and too young to understand that a woman was not meant to be understood. And he wanted her. That wasn't new, but the desire had come with surprising speed and surprising force.

Rebecca Malone might have started out as an impulse, but she was now a mystery. One he intended to solve. With a little laugh, he bent to scoop up the shoes she'd forgotten. He hadn't felt quite so alive in months.

CHAPTER 2

Stephen wasn't the kind of man who rearranged his schedule to spend the day with a woman. Especially a woman he barely knew. He was a wealthy man, but he was also a busy man, driven by both pride and ambition to maintain a high level of involvement in all his projects. He shouldered responsibility well and had learned to enjoy the benefits of hard work and dedication.

His time on Corfu wasn't free—or rather hadn't been planned as free. Mixing business and pleasure wasn't his style. He pursued both, separately, with utter concentration. Yet he found himself juggling appointments, meetings, conference calls, in order to have the afternoon open for Rebecca.

He supposed any man would want to get to know a woman who flirted easily over a champagne flute one moment and dived fully dressed into the sea the next.

"I've postponed your meeting with Theoharis until five-thirty this evening." Stephen's secretary scribbled on a notepad she had resting on her lap. "He will meet you for early cocktails in the suite. I've arranged for hors d'oeuvres and a bottle of ouzo."

"Always efficient, Elana."

She smiled and tucked a fall of dark hair behind her ear. "I try."

When Stephen rose to pace to the window, she folded her hands and waited. She had worked for him for five years, she admired his energy and his business acumen, and—fortunately for both of them—had long since gotten over an early crush. There was often speculation about their personal relationship, but though he could be friendly—even kind when it suited him—with Stephen, business was business.

"Contact Mithos in Athens. Have him fax that report by the end of the day. And I want to hear from Lereau by five, Paris time."

"Shall I call and give him a nudge?"

"If you think it's necessary." Restless, he dug his hands in his pockets. Where had this sudden discontent come from? he wondered. He was wealthy, successful, and free, as always, to move from place to place. As he stared out at the sea, he remembered the scent of Rebecca's skin. "Send flowers to Rebecca Malone's suite. Wildflowers, nothing formal. This afternoon."

Elana made a note, hoping she'd get a look at this Rebecca Malone before long. She had already heard through the grapevine that Stephen had had dinner with an American woman. "And the card?"

He wasn't a man for poetry. "Just my name."

"Anything else?"

"Yes." He turned and offered her a half smile. "Take some time off. Go to the beach."

Pad in hand, she rose. "I'll be sure to work it in. Enjoy your afternoon, Stephen."

He intended to. As she left him, Stephen glanced at his watch. It was fifteen minutes before eleven. There was work he could do to fill in the time, a quick call that could be made. Instead, he picked up Rebecca's shoes.

After three tries, Rebecca settled on an outfit. She didn't have an abundance of clothes, because she'd preferred to spend her funds on travel. But she had splurged here and there on her route through Europe. No tidy CPA suits, she thought as she tied a vivid fuchsia sash at the waist of her sapphire-colored cotton pants. No sensible shoes or pastel blouses. The last shock of color came from a primrose-hued blouse cut generously to layer over a skinny tank top in the same shade as the slacks.

The combination delighted her, if only because her firm had preferred quiet colors and clean lines.

She had no idea where she was going, and she didn't care.

It was a beautiful day, even though she'd awoken with a dull headache from the champagne, and the disorientation that went with it. A light, early breakfast on her terrace and a quick dip in the sea had cleared both away. She still had trouble believing that she could lounge through a morning as she pleased—and that she'd spent the evening with a man she'd just met.

Aunt Jeannie would have tut-tutted and reminded her of the dangers of being a woman alone. Some of her friends would have been shocked, others envious. But they would all have been astonished that steady Rebecca had strolled in the moonlight with a gorgeous man with a scar on his jawline and eyes like velvet.

If she hadn't had his jacket as proof, she might have thought she'd dreamed it. There had never been anything wrong with her imagination—just the application of it. Often she'd pictured herself in an exotic place with an exotic man, with moonlight and music. Imagined herself, she remembered. And then she'd turned on her calculator and gotten down to business.

But she hadn't dreamed this. She could still remember the giddy, half-terrified feeling that had swarmed through her when he'd gathered her close. When his mouth had been only an inch from hers and the sea and the champagne had roared in her head.

What if he had kissed her? What tastes would she have found? Rich, strong ones, she mused, almost able to savor them as she traced a fingertip over her lips. After just one evening she was absolutely certain there would be nothing lukewarm about Stephen Nickodemus. She wasn't nearly so certain about Rebecca.

She probably would have fumbled and blushed and stammered. With a shake of her head, she pulled a brush through her hair. Exciting men didn't tumble all over themselves to kiss neat, practical-minded women.

But he'd asked to see her again.

Rebecca wasn't certain whether she was disappointed or relieved that he hadn't pressed his advantage and kissed her. She'd been kissed before, held before, of course. But she had a feeling—a very definite feeling— that it wouldn't be the same with Stephen. He might make her want more, offer more, than she had with any other man.

Crossing bridges too soon, she decided as she checked the contents of her big straw bag. She wasn't going to have an affair with him, or with anyone. Even the new, improved Rebecca Malone wasn't the type for a casual affair. But maybe— She caught her lower lip between her teeth. If the time was right she might have a romance she'd remember long after she left Greece.

For now, she was ready, but it was much too early to go down. It would hardly make her look like a well-traveled woman of the world if she popped down to the lobby and paced for ten minutes. This was her fantasy, after all. She didn't want him to think she was inexperienced and overeager.

Only the knock on the door prevented her from changing her mind about her outfit one more time.

"Hello." Stephen studied her for a moment, unsmiling. He'd nearly been certain he'd exaggerated, but she was just as vibrant, just as exciting, in the morning as she had been in the moonlight. He held out her shoes. "I thought you might need these."

She laughed, remembering her impulsive dunk in the sea. "I didn't realize I'd left them on the beach. Come in a minute." With a neatness ingrained in her from childhood, she turned to take them to the bedroom closet. "I'm ready to go if you are."

Stephen lifted a brow. He preferred promptness, but he never expected it in anyone but a business associate. "I've got a Jeep waiting. Some of the roads are rough."

"Sounds great." Rebecca came out again, carrying her bag and a flat-brimmed straw hat. She handed Stephen his jacket, neatly folded. "I forgot to give this back to you last night." Should she offer to have it cleaned? she wondered when he only continued to look at her. Fiddling with the strap of her bag, she decided against it. "Does taking pictures bother you?"

"No, why?"

"Good, because I take lots of them. I can't seem to stop myself."

She wasn't kidding. As Stephen drove up into the hills, she took shots of everything. Sheep, tomato plants, olive groves and straggly sage. He stopped so that she could walk out near the edge of a cliff and look down at a small village huddled near the sea.

She wouldn't be able to capture it on film; she wasn't clever enough. But she knew she'd never forget that light, so pure, so clear, or the contrast between the orange tiled roofs and the low white-washed walls and the deep, dangerous blue of the water that flung itself against the weathered rock that rose into harsh crags. A stork, legs tucked, glided over the water, where fishing boats bobbed.

There were nets drying on the beach and children playing. Flowers bloomed and tangled where the wind had planted them, more spectacular than any planned arrangement could ever be.

"It's beautiful." Her throat tightened with emotion, and with a longing she couldn't have defined. "So calm. You imagine women baking black bread and the men coming home smelling of fish and the sea. It looks as though it hasn't changed in a hundred years."

"Very little." He glanced down himself, surprised and more than a little pleased that she would be touched by something so simple. "We cling to antiquity."

"I haven't seen the Acropolis yet, but I don't think it could be any more spectacular than this." She lifted her face, delighted by the way the wind whipped at it. Here, high above the sea, she absorbed everything—the salty, rough-edged bite of the wind, the clarity of color and sound, and the man beside her. Letting her camera dangle from its strap, she turned to him. "I haven't thanked you for taking the time to show me all of this."

He took her hand, not to raise it to his lips, just to hold it. It was a link he hadn't known he wanted. "I'm enjoying seeing the familiar through someone else's eyes. Your eyes."

Suddenly the edge of the cliff seemed too close, the sun too hot. Could he do that just by touching her? With an effort, Rebecca smiled, keeping her voice light. "If you ever come to Philadelphia, I'll do the same for you."

It was odd. She'd looked almost frightened for a moment. Fragile and frightened. Stephen had always carefully avoided women who were easily bruised. "I'll consider that a promise."

They continued to drive, over roads that jarred and climbed and twisted. She saw her first of the *agrimi*, the wild goat of Greece, and the rocky pastures dotted with sturdy sheep. And everywhere, rich and defiant, was the intense color of flowers.

He didn't complain when she asked him to stop so

that she could snap pictures of tiny blue star blossoms that pushed their way through cracks in the rock. He listened to her delight as she framed a thick, thorny stem topped with a ragged yellow flower. It made him realize, and regret, that it had been years since he'd taken the time to look closely at the small, vital things that grew around him.

He looked now at Rebecca standing in the sunlight, her hat fluttering around her face and her laugh dancing on the air.

Often the road clung to cliffs that plunged dizzily into the sea. Rebecca, who was too timid to fight rush-hour traffic, found it exhilarating.

She felt almost like another person. She *was* another person, she thought, laughing as she held on to her hat to keep the wind from snatching it away.

"I love it!" she shouted over the wind and the noise of the engine. "It's wild and old and incredible. Like no place I've ever been."

Still laughing, she lifted her camera and snapped his picture as he drove. He wore sunglasses with amber lenses and had a cigar clamped between his teeth. The wind blew through his hair and chased the smoke behind them. He stopped the Jeep, took the camera and snapped a picture of her in turn.

"Hungry?"

She dragged her tousled hair back from her face. "Starving."

He leaned over to open her door. A current passed through her, sharp and electric, strong enough to make him pause with his arm across her body and his face close to hers. It was there again, he thought as he waited and watched. The awareness, ripe and seductive. And the innocence, as alluring as it was contradictory. In a test—a test for both of them—he lifted a hand to stroke her cheek. It was as soft as her scent.

"Are you afraid of me, Rebecca?"

"No." That was true; she was nearly sure of it. "Should I be?"

He didn't smile. Through the amber lenses she saw that his eyes were very intense. "I'm not entirely sure." When he pulled away he heard her release an unsteady breath. He wasn't feeling completely steady himself. "We'll have to walk a little first."

Confused, her mind churning, she stepped out onto the dirt path. A woman on a simple date didn't tremble every time a man got close, Rebecca told herself as Stephen lifted the picnic basket out of the back. She was behaving like a teenager, not a grown woman.

Troubled by his own thoughts, Stephen stopped beside her. He hesitated, then held out a hand. It felt good, simply good, when she put hers in it.

They walked through an olive grove in a companionable silence while the sun streamed down on dusty leaves and rocky ground. There was no sound of the sea here, but when the wind was right she could hear the screech of a gull far away. The island was small, but here it seemed uninhabited.

"I haven't had a picnic in years." Rebecca spread the cloth. "And never in an olive grove." She glanced around, wanting to remember every leaf and pebble. "Are we trespassing?"

"No." Stephen took a bottle of white wine from the basket. Rebecca left him to it and started rummaging in search of food.

"Do you know the owner?"

"I'm the owner." He drew the cork with a gentle pop.

"Oh." She looked around again. It should have occurred to her that he would own something impressive, different, exciting. "It sounds romantic. Owning an olive grove."

He lifted a brow. He owned a number of them, but he had never thought of them as romantic. They were simply profitable. He offered her a glass, then tapped it with his own. "To romance, then."

She swept down her lashes, battling shyness. To Stephen, the gesture was only provocative. "I hope you're hungry," she began, knowing she was talking too fast. "It all looks wonderful." She took a quick sip of wine to ease her dry throat, then set it aside to finish unpacking the basket.

There were sweet black olives as big as a man's

thumb, and there was a huge slab of sharp cheese. There were cold lamb and hunks of bread, and fruit so fresh it could have been just plucked from the stem.

Gradually she began to relax again.

"You've told me very little about yourself." Stephen topped off her wine and watched her bite into a ripe red plum. "I know little more than that you come from Philadelphia and enjoy traveling."

What could she tell him? A man like him was bound to be bored with the life story of the painfully ordinary Rebecca Malone. Lies had never come easily to her, so she skirted between fact and fiction. "There's little more. I grew up in Philadelphia. I lost both of my parents when I was a teenager, and I lived with my aunt Jeannie. She was very dear, and she made the loss bearable."

"It's painful." He flicked his lighter at the end of a cigar, remembering not only the pain, but also the fury he had felt when his father had died and left him orphaned at sixteen. "It steals childhood."

"Yes." So he understood that. It made her feel close to him, close and comfortable. "Maybe that's why I like to travel. Every time you see a new place you can be a child again."

"So you don't look for roots?"

She glanced at him then. He was leaning back against the trunk of a tree, smoking lazily, watching carefully. "I don't know what I'm looking for."

"Is there a man?"

She moved her shoulders, determined not to be embarrassed. "No."

He took her hand, drawing her closer. "No one?"

"No, I…" She wasn't certain what she would have said, but could say nothing at all when he turned her palm upward and pressed his lips to its center. She felt the fire burst there, in her hand, then race everywhere.

"You're very responsive, Rebecca." He lowered her hand but kept it in his. He could feel the heat, but he wasn't sure whether it had sprung to her skin or to his own. "If there's no one, the men in your Philadelphia must be very slow."

"I've been too…busy."

His lips curved at that. There was a tremor in her voice, and there was passion in her eyes. "Busy?"

"Yes." Afraid she'd make a fool of herself, she drew her hand back. "This was wonderful." Trying to calm herself, she pushed a hand through her hair. "You know what I need?"

"No. Tell me."

"Another picture." She sprang to her feet and, steadier, grinned. "A memento of my first picnic in an olive grove. Let's see…you can stand right over there. The sun's good in front of that tree, and I should be able to frame in that section of the grove."

Amused, Stephen tapped out his cigar. "How much more film do you have?"

"This is the last roll—but I have scads back at the hotel." She flicked him a quick laughing glance. "I warned you."

"So you did." Competent hands, he thought as he watched her focus and adjust. He hadn't realized he could be as attracted to competence as he was to beauty. She mumbled to herself, tossing her head back so that her hair swung, then settled. His stomach tightened without warning.

Good God, he wanted her. She'd done nothing to make him burn and strain this way. He couldn't accuse her of taunting or teasing, and yet...he felt taunted. He felt teased. For the first time in his life he felt totally seduced by a woman who had done nothing more than give him a few smiles and a little companionship.

Even now she was chattering away as she secured her camera to the limb of a tree. Talking easily, as though they were just friends, as though she felt nothing more than a light, unimportant affection. But he'd seen it. Stephen felt his blood heat as he remembered the quick flash of arousal he'd seen on her face. He'd see it again. And more.

"I'm going to set the timer," Rebecca went on, blissfully unaware of Stephen's thoughts. "All you have to do is stand there. Once I get this damn thing set, I'm going to run over so it'll take one of both—There." She interrupted herself, crossed her fingers and ran to Stephen's side in a dash. "Unless I messed up, it'll snap all by itself in—"

The rest of the words slid down her throat as he crushed her against him and captured her mouth.

CHAPTER 3

Heat. Light. Speed. Rebecca felt them, felt each separate, distinct sensation. Urgency. Demand. Impatience. She tasted them, as clearly as wild honey, on his lips. Though she'd never experienced it, she had known exactly what it would be like to be with him, mouth to mouth and need to need.

In an instant the world had narrowed from what could be seen and understood to a pure, seamless blanket of emotion. It cloaked her, not softly, not in comfort, but tightly, hotly, irresistibly. Caught between fear and delight, she lifted a hand to his cheek.

God, she was sweet. Even as he dragged her closer, aroused by the simplicity of her acceptance, he was struck by—disarmed by—her sweetness. There had been a hesitation, almost too brief to be measured, before her lips had parted beneath his. Parted, invited, accepted.

There was a sigh, so soft it could barely be heard, as she stroked her hands up his back to his shoulders. Curious, simple, generous. A man could drown in such sweetness, fall prisoner to such pliancy. And be saved by it. Beneath the patterned shade of the olive tree, she gave him more than passion. She gave him hope.

Charmed, he murmured some careless Greek phrase lovers might exchange. The words meant nothing to her, but the sound of them on the still air, the feel of them stroking across her lips…seduction. Glorious seduction.

Pleasure burst in her blood, in her head, in her heart, thousands of tiny bubbles of it, until she was straining against him.

The quiet explosion rocked him. It tightened his chest, fuddled his mind. She fitted into his arms as if she'd been born for him. As if, somehow, they had known each other before, loved before, hungered before. Something seemed to erupt between them, something molten, powerful, dangerous. But it wasn't new. It was ancient, a whispering echo of ageless passions.

She began to tremble. How could this be so right, so familiar? It wasn't possible to feel safe and threatened at the same time. But she did. She clung to him while a dim, floating image danced through her head. She had kissed him before. Just like this. As her mind spun, she heard her own mindless murmurs answer his. As freely, as inescapably as the sun poured light, response flowed from her. She couldn't stop it. Frightened by her sudden loss of control, she struggled against him, against herself.

He slipped his hands up to her shoulders, but not to free her, to look at her. To look at how their coming together had changed her. It had changed him. Passion had made her eyes heavy, seductive. Fear had clouded them. Her lips were full, softened and parted by his. Her breath shivered through them. Under his hands he could feel the heat of her skin and the quick, involuntary trembling of her muscles.

No pretense here, he decided as he studied her. He was holding both innocence and delight in his hands.

"Stephen, I—"

"Again."

Then his face filled her vision and she was lost.

Differently. Should she have known that one man could hold one woman in so many different ways? That one man could kiss one woman with such stunning variety? There was gentleness now, as familiar and as novel as the urgency. His lips persuaded rather than demanded. They savored instead of devouring. Her surrender came as quietly, and as unmistakably, as her earlier passion. The trembling stopped; the fear vanished. With a complete trust that surprised them both, she leaned against him, giving.

More aroused by her serenity than by the storm that had come before, Stephen pulled back. He had to, or what had begun would finish without either of them saying a word. As he swore and pulled out a cigar, Rebecca placed a hand on the olive tree for support.

Moments, she thought. It had been only moments, and yet she felt as though years had passed, racing backward or forward, perhaps spinning in circles. In a place like this, with a man like this, what difference did it make what year it was? What century?

Half terrified, she lifted a hand to her lips. Despite her fear, they curved under her touch. She could still taste him. Still feel him. And nothing, nothing, would ever be quite the same again.

He stared out at the rough and dusty land he'd known as a boy, and beyond, to the stark, tumbling rocks where he and other wild things had climbed.

What was he doing with her? Furious with himself, he drew on the cigar. What was he feeling? It was new, and far from comfortable. And it was comfort he preferred, he reminded himself. Comfort and freedom. Bringing himself under control, he turned to her again, determined to treat what had happened as a man should—lightly.

She just stood there, with the sun and the shade falling over her. There was neither recrimination nor invitation in her eyes. She didn't flinch or step forward, but merely stood, watching him with the faintest of smiles, as if... As if, Stephen realized, she knew what questions he was asking himself—and the answers.

"It grows late."

She felt the ache and fought not to let it show on her face. "I guess you're right." She dragged a hand through her hair—it was the first sign of her agitation—then walked over to pick up her camera. "I should have a picture to remember all this by," she said, forcing brightness into her voice. Her breath caught when his fingers closed over her arm and whirled her around.

"Who are you?" he demanded. "What are you?"

"I don't know what you mean." The emotion burst out before she could stop it. "I don't know what you want."

With one jerk he had her tumbling against him. "You know what I want."

Her heart was in her throat, beating wildly. She found it strange that it was not fear but desire that she felt. She hadn't known she was capable of feeling a need that was so unreasonable, so reckless. It was almost purifying to experience it, and to see it mirrored in his eyes.

"It takes more than one afternoon." Didn't it? Her voice rose as she tried to convince herself. "It takes more than a picnic and a walk in the moonlight for me."

"One moment the temptress, the next the outraged innocent. Do you do it to intrigue me, Rebecca?" She shook her head, and his fingers tightened. "It works," he murmured. "You've hardly been out of my mind since I first saw you. I want to make love with you, here, in the sun."

Color flooded her face, not because she was embarrassed, but because she could imagine it, perfectly. And then what? Carefully she leveled her breathing. Whatever impulses she had followed, whatever bridges she had burned, she still needed answers.

"No." It cost her to go against her own needs and say it. "Not when I'm unsure and you're angry." She took a deep breath and kept her eyes on him. "You're hurting me, Stephen. I don't think you mean to."

Slowly he released her arm. He was angry, furious, but not at her refusal. The anger stemmed from the need she pulled from him, a need that had come too fast and too strong for him to channel. "We'll go back."

Rebecca merely nodded, then knelt to gather the remains of the picnic.

He was a busy man, much too busy to brood about a woman he barely knew and didn't understand at all. That was what Stephen told himself. He had reports to read, calls to make and paperwork—which he had both a talent and a distaste for—to deal with. A couple of simple kisses weren't enough to take a man's mind off his work.

But there hadn't been anything simple about them.

Disgusted, Stephen pushed away from his desk and wandered to the terrace doors. He'd left them open because the breeze, and the fragrances it brought, helped him forget he was obligated to be inside.

For days he'd worked his way through his responsibilities, trying to ignore the nagging itch at the back of his mind—the itch that was Rebecca. There was no reason for him to stay on Corfu. He could have handled his business in Athens, or Crete, or in London, for that matter. Still, he'd made no plans to leave, though he'd also made no attempt to approach her.

She…concerned him, he decided. To be drawn to an attractive woman was as natural as breathing. To have the attraction cause discomfort, confusion, even annoyance was anything but natural. A taste of her hadn't been enough. Yet he hesitated.

She was…mysterious. Perhaps that was why he couldn't push her from his mind. On the surface she appeared to be an attractive, free-spirited woman who grabbed life with both hands. Yet there were undercurrents. The hints of innocence, of shyness. The sweetness. The complexity of her kept him wondering, thinking, imagining.

Perhaps that was her trick. Women had them…were entitled to them. It was a waste of time to begrudge them their illusions and their feminine magic. More than a waste of time, it was foolish, when a man could enjoy the benefits. But there was more, and somehow less, to Rebecca than innate feminine magic.

When he had kissed her, though it had been the first time, it had been like coming back to a lover, to a love, after a painful separation. When his lips had found hers, something had filled him. A heat, an impatience, a knowledge.

He knew her, knew more than her name and her background and the color of her eyes. He knew all of her. Yet he knew nothing.

Fantasies, he told himself. He didn't have time for them. Leaning a hip against the railing, he lit a cigar and watched the sea.

As always, it pulled at him, bringing back memories of a childhood that had been careless and too short. There were times, rare times, when he allowed himself to regret. Times when the sun was a white flash of heat and the water was blue and endless. His father had taught him a great deal. How to fish, how to see both beauty and excitement in new places, how to drink like a man.

Fifteen years, Stephen thought, a smile ghosting around his mouth. He still missed him, missed the companionship, the robust laughter. They had been friends, as well as parent and child, with a bond as easy, and as strong, as any Stephen had ever known. But his father had died as he would have wanted to, at sea and in his prime.

He would have taken one look at Rebecca, rolled his

eyes, kissed his fingers and urged his son to enjoy. But Stephen wasn't the boy he had once been. He was more cautious, more aware of consequences. If a man dived into the sea, he should know the depth and the currents.

Then he saw her, coming from the sea. Water ran down her body, glistening in the strong sun, sparkling against skin that had warmed in the last few days to a dusky gold. As he looked, as he wanted, he felt his muscles clench, one by one, shoulders, stomach, thighs. Without his being aware, his fingers tightened, snapping the cigar in two. He hadn't known that desire could arouse a reaction so akin to anger.

She stopped, and though he knew she was unaware of him, she might easily have been posing. To taunt, to tease, to invite. As drops of water slid down her, she stretched, lifting her face skyward. Her skimpy suit rested low over her boyish hips, shifted enticingly over the subtle curve of her breasts. At that moment, she was totally absorbed in her own pleasure and as unself-conscious as any young animal standing in the sun. Nothing had ever been so alluring.

Then, slowly, seductively, she combed her fingers through her hair, smiling, as if she enjoyed the wet, silky feel of it. Watching her, he felt the air back up and clog in his lungs. He could have murdered her for it, for making him want so unreasonably what he did not yet understand.

She plucked a long, mannish T-shirt from a straw bag and, after tugging it on, strolled barefoot into the hotel.

He stood there, waiting for the need to pass. But it built, layered with an ache that infuriated him and a longing that baffled him.

He should ignore her. Instinct warned him that if he didn't his life would never be the same. She was nothing more than a distraction, a momentary impulse he should resist. He should turn away, go back to work. He had commitments, obligations, and no time to waste on fantasies. With an oath, he tossed the broken cigar over the rail.

There were times, he thought, when a man had to trust in fate and dive in.

CHAPTER 4

Rebecca had hardly shut the door behind her before she turned back to answer the knock. The sun and the water had left her pleasantly tired, but all thoughts of a lazy catnap vanished when she saw Stephen.

He looked wonderful. Cool, a little windblown, intense. For days she'd wondered about him, wondered and wished. She felt her pulse skip and her lips curve just at the sight of him. With an effort, she kept her voice breezy.

"Hello. I wasn't sure you were still on the island."

It wasn't really a lie, she told herself. An offhand inquiry had assured her that Mr. Nickodemus hadn't checked out, but she hadn't actually seen him.

"I saw you come up from the beach."

"Oh." Unconsciously she tugged at the hem of her cover-up. To Stephen the small gesture was one more contradictory signal. "I can't seem to get enough of the sun and the sea. Would you like to come in?"

By way of an answer he stepped through and shut the door behind him. It made a very quiet, a very final sound. Rebecca's carefully built poise began to crumble. "I never thanked you for the flowers." She made a gesture indicating the vase near the window, then brought her hands back together and linked them in front of her. "They're still beautiful. I…I thought I might run into you, in the dining room, on the beach, or…" Her words trailed off when he lifted a hand to her hair.

"I've been busy." He watched her eyes, eyes that were as clear as rainwater, blur at the slight touch. "Business."

It was ridiculous, she knew, but she wasn't at all sure she could speak. "If you have to work, I doubt you could pick a more beautiful place."

He stepped closer. She smelled of the water and the sun. "You're enjoying the resort, and the island."

Her hand was in his now, caught lightly. It took only that to make her knees weak. "Yes, very much."

"Perhaps you'd like to see it from a different perspective." Deliberately, wanting to test them both, he lifted her hand to his lips. He grazed her knuckles—it was barely a whisper of contact—and felt the jolt. She felt it, and he could see that she did, so it couldn't just be his imagination. "Spend the day with me tomorrow on my boat."

"What?"

He smiled, delighted with her response. "Will you come with me?"

Anywhere. Astonished, she stepped back. "I haven't any plans."

"Good." He closed the distance between them again. Her hands fluttered up in flustered defense, then settled again when he made no attempt to touch her. "Then I'll make them for you. I'll come for you in the morning. Nine?"

A boat. He'd said something about a boat. Rebecca drew in a deep breath and tried to pull herself together. This wasn't like her—going off into daydreams, feeling weak-kneed, being flooded with waves of desire. And it felt wonderful.

"I'd like that." She gave him what she hoped was an easy woman-of-the-world smile.

"Until tomorrow, then." He started for the door, then turned, a hand on the knob. "Rebecca, don't forget your camera."

She waited until he'd closed the door before she spun in three quick circles.

When Stephen had said "boat," Rebecca had pictured a trim little cabin cruiser. Instead, she stepped onto the glossy mahogany deck of a streamlined hundred-foot yacht.

"You could live on this," Rebecca said, then wished she'd bitten her tongue. But he only laughed.

"I often do."

"Welcome aboard, sir," a white-uniformed man with a British accent said.

"Grady. This is my guest, Miss Malone."

"Ma'am." Grady's cool British reserve didn't flicker for an instant, but Rebecca felt herself being summed up.

"Cast off when you're ready." Stephen took Rebecca's arm. "Would you like a tour?"

"Yes." A yacht. She was on a yacht. It took all her willpower to keep her camera in the bag. "I'd love to see it all."

He took her below, through four elegantly appointed cabins. Her comment about living on board had been said impulsively, but she could see now that it could be done easily, even luxuriously.

Above there was a large glassed-in cabin in which one could stretch out comfortably, out of the sun, and watch the sea, whatever the weather. She had known that there were people who lived like this. Part of her job had been to research and calculate so that those who did paid the government as little as possible. But to be there, to see it, to be surrounded by it, was entirely different from adding figures on paper.

There was a masculine feel to the cabin, to the entire boat—leather, wood, muted colors. There were shelves filled with books and a fully stocked bar, as well as a stereo system.

"All the comforts of home," Rebecca murmured, but she'd noted that there were doors and panels that could be secured in case of rough weather. What would it be like to ride out a storm at sea, to watch the rain lash the windows and feel the deck heave?

She gave a quick gasp when she felt the floor move. Stephen took her arm again to steady her.

"We're under way." Curious, he turned her to face him. "Are you afraid of boats?"

"No." She could hardly admit that the biggest one she'd been on before this had been a two-passenger canoe at summer camp. "It just startled me." Under way, she thought as she prayed that her system would settle. It was such an exciting, adventurous word. "Can we go out on deck? I'd like to watch."

It was exciting. She felt it the moment the wind hit her face and rushed through her hair. At the rail, she leaned out, delighted to see the island shrink and the sea spread. Because she couldn't resist and he didn't laugh at her, she took half a dozen pictures as the boat sped away from land.

"It's better than flying," she decided. "You feel a part of it. Look." With a laugh, she pointed. "The birds are chasing us."

Stephen didn't bother to glance at the gulls that

wheeled and called above the boat's wake. He preferred to watch the delight and excitement bloom on her face. "Do you always enjoy so completely?"

"Yes." She tossed her hair away from her face, only to have the wind rush it back again. With another laugh, she stretched back from the railing, her face lifted to the sun. "Oh, yes."

Irresistible. With his hands at her waist, he spun her toward him. It was like holding a live wire. The shock rippled from her to him, then back again. "Everything?" His fingers spread over her back and, with the slightest pressure, moved her forward until their thighs met.

"I don't know." Instinctively she braced her hands on his shoulders. "I haven't tried everything." But she wanted to. Held close, with the sound of the water and the wind, she wanted to. Without giving a thought to self-preservation, she leaned toward him.

He swore, lightly, under his breath. Rebecca jolted back as if he had shouted at her. Stephen caught her hand as he nodded to the steward, who had just approached with drinks. "Thank you, Victor. Just leave everything." His voice was smooth enough, but Rebecca felt the tension in his hand as he led her to a chair.

He probably thought she was a fool, she decided. All but tumbling into his arms every time he touched her. He was obviously a man of the world—and a kind man, she added as she sipped her mimosa. Not all powerful men spoke kindly to those who worked for them. Her lips curved, a little wryly, as she sipped again. She knew that firsthand.

His body was in turmoil. Stephen couldn't remember, even in his youth, having had a woman affect him so irrationally. He knew how to persuade, how to seduce— and always with finesse. But whenever he was around this woman for more than five minutes he felt like a stallion being spurred and curbed at the same time.

And he was fascinated. Fascinated by the ease with which she went into his arms, by the trust he saw when he looked down into her eyes. As he had in the olive grove, he found himself believing he'd looked into those eyes, those rainwater-clear eyes, a hundred times before.

Still churning, he took out a cigar. The thought was fanciful, but his desire was very real. If there couldn't be finesse, perhaps there could be candor.

"I want you, Rebecca."

She felt her heart stop, then start up again with slow, dull throbs. Carefully she took another sip, then cleared her throat. "I know." It amazed her, flattered her, terrified her.

She seemed so cool. He envied her. "Will you come with me, to my cabin?"

She looked at him then. Her heart and her head were giving very different answers. It sounded so easy, so…natural. If there was a man she could give herself to, wholly, he was with her now. Complications, what complications there were, were her own.

But no matter how far she had run from Philadelphia and her own strict upbringing, there were still lines she couldn't cross.

"I can't."

"Can't?" He lit his cigar, astonished that they were discussing making love as though it were as casual a choice as what dinner entrée to choose. "Or won't?"

She drew a breath. Her palms were damp on the glass, and she set it down. "Can't. I want to." Her eyes, huge and lake-pale, clung to his. "I very much want to, but…"

"But?"

"I know so little about you." She picked up her glass again because her empty hands tended to twist together. "Hardly more than your name, that you own an olive grove and like the sea. It's not enough."

"Then I'll tell you more."

She relaxed enough to smile. "I don't know what to ask."

He leaned back in his chair, the tension dissolving as quickly as it had built. She could do that to him with nothing more than a smile. He knew no one who could excite and solace with so little effort.

"Do you believe in fate, Rebecca? In something unexpected, even unlooked-for, often a small thing that completely and irrevocably changes one's life?"

She thought of her aunt's death and her own uncharacteristic decisions. "Yes. Yes, I do."

"Good." His gaze skimmed over her face, quickly, then more leisurely. "I'd nearly forgotten that I believe it, too. Then I saw you, sitting alone."

There were ways and ways to seduce, she was discovering. A look, a tone, could be every bit as devastating as a caress. She wanted him more in that moment than she had ever known she could want anything. To give herself time, and distance, she rose and walked to the rail.

Even her silence aroused him. She had said she knew too little about him. He knew even less of her. And he didn't care. It was dangerous, possibly even destructive, but he didn't care. As he watched her with the wind billowing her shirt and her hair he realized that he didn't give a damn about where she had come from, where she had been, what she had done.

When lightning strikes, it destroys, though it blazes with power. Rising, he went to her and stood, as she did, facing the sea.

"When I was young, very young," he began, "there was another moment that changed things. My father was a man for the water. He lived for it. Died for it." When he went on it was almost as if he were speaking to himself now, remembering. Rebecca turned her head to look at him. "I was ten or eleven. Everything was going well, the nets were full. My father and I were walking along the beach. He stopped, dipped his hand into the water, made a fist and opened it. 'You can't hold it,' he said to me. 'No matter how you try or how you love or how you sweat.' Then he dug into the sand. It was wet and clung together in his hand. 'But this,' he said, 'a man can hold.' We never spoke of it again. When my time came, I turned my back on the sea and held the land."

"It was right for you."

"Yes." He lifted a hand to catch at the ends of her hair. "It was right. Such big, quiet eyes you have, Rebecca," he murmured. "Have they seen enough, I wonder, to know what's right for you?"

"I guess I've been a little slow in starting to look." Her blood was pounding thickly. She would have stepped back, but he shifted so that she was trapped between him and the rail.

"You tremble when I touch you." He slid his hands up her arms, then down until their hands locked. "Have you any idea how exciting that is?"

Her chest tightened, diminishing her air even as the muscles in her legs went limp. "Stephen, I meant it when I said…" He brushed his lips gently over her temple. "I can't. I need to…" He feathered a kiss along her jawline, softly. "To think."

He felt her fingers go lax in his. She was suddenly fragile, outrageously vulnerable, irresistibly tempting. "When I kissed you the first time I gave you no choice." His lips trailed over her face, light as a whisper, circling, teasing, avoiding her mouth. "You have one now."

He was hardly touching her. A breath, a whisper, a mere promise of a touch. The slow, subtle passage of his lips over her skin couldn't have been called a kiss, could never have been called a demand. She had only to push away to end the torment. And the glory.

A choice? Had he told her she had a choice? "No, I don't," she murmured as she turned to find his lips with hers.

No choice, no past, no future. Only now. She felt the present, with all its needs and hungers, well up inside her. The kiss was instantly hot, instantly desperate. His heart pounded fast and hard against hers, thunderous now, as he twisted a hand in her hair to pull her head back. To plunder. No one had ever taken her like this. No one had ever warned her that a touch of violence could be so exciting. Her gasp of surprise turned into a moan of pleasure as his tongue skimmed over hers.

He thought of lightning bolts again, thought of that flash of power and light. She was electric in his arms, sparking, sizzling. Her scent, as soft, as seductive, as a whisper, clouded his mind, even as the taste of her heightened his appetite.

She was all woman, she was every woman, and yet she was like no other. He could hear each quick catch of her breath above the roar of the motor. With her name on his lips, he pressed them to the vulnerable line of her throat, where the skin was heated from the sun and as delicate as water.

She might have slid bonelessly to the deck if his body hadn't pressed hers so firmly against the rail. In wonder, in panic, she felt his muscles turn to iron wherever they touched her. Never before had she felt so fragile, so at the mercy of her own desires. The sea was as calm as glass, but she felt herself tossed, tumbled, wrecked. With a sigh that was almost a sob, she wrapped her arms around him.

It was the defenselessness of the gesture that pulled him back from the edge. He must have been mad. For a moment he'd been close, much too close, to dragging her down to the deck without a thought to her wishes or to the consequences. With his eyes closed, he held her, feeling the erratic beat of her heart, hearing her shallow, shuddering breath.

Perhaps he was still mad, Stephen thought. Even as the ragged edges of desire eased, something deeper and far more dangerous bloomed.

He wanted her, in a way no man could safely want a woman. Forever.

Fate, he thought again as he stroked her hair. It seemed he was falling in love whether he wished it or not. A few hours with her and he felt more than he had ever imagined he could feel.

There had been a few times in his life when he had seen and desired on instinct alone. What he had seen and desired, he had taken. Just as he would take her. But when he took, he meant to keep.

Carefully he stepped back. "Maybe neither of us has a choice." He dipped his hands into his pockets. "And if I touch you again, here, now, I won't give you one."

Unable to pretend, knowing they were shaking, she pushed her hands through her hair. She didn't bother to disguise the tremor in her voice. She wouldn't have known how. "I won't want one." She saw his eyes darken quickly, dangerously, but she didn't know his hands were balled into fists, straining.

"You make it difficult for me."

A long, shuddering breath escaped her. No one had ever wanted her this way. Probably no one ever would again. "I'm sorry. I don't mean to."

"No." Deliberately he relaxed his hands. "I don't think you do. That's one of the things about you I find most intriguing. I will have you, Rebecca." He saw something flicker in her eyes.... Excitement? Panic? A combination of the two, perhaps. "Because I'm sure of it, because I know you're sure of it, I'll do my best to give you a little more time."

Her natural humor worked through the sliver of unease she felt. "I'm not sure whether I should thank you politely or run like hell."

He grinned, surprising himself, then flicked a finger down her cheek. "I wouldn't advise running, *matia mou*. I'd only catch you."

She was sure of that, too. One look at his face, even with the smile that softened it, and she knew. Kind, yes, but with a steely underlying ruthlessness. "Then I'll go with the thank-you."

"You're welcome." Patience, he realized, would have to be developed. And quickly. "Would you like to swim? There's a bay. We're nearly there."

The water might, just might, cool her off. "I'd love it."

CHAPTER 5

The water was cool and mirror-clear. Rebecca lowered herself into it with a sigh of pure pleasure. Back in Philadelphia she would have been at her desk, calculator clicking, the jacket of her neat business suit carefully smoothed over the back of her chair. Her figures would always tally, her forms would always be properly filed.

The dependable, efficient Miss Malone.

Instead, she was swimming in a crystal-clear bay, letting the water cool and the sun heat. Ledgers and accounts were worlds away. Here, as close as a handspan, was a man who was teaching her everything she would ever want to know about needs, desires, and the fragility of the heart.

He couldn't know it, she thought. She doubted she'd ever have the courage to tell him that he was the only one who had ever made her tremble and burn. A man as physically aware as he would only be uncomfortable knowing he held an inexperienced woman in his arms.

The water lapped around her with a sound as quiet as her own sigh. But he didn't know, because when she was in his arms she didn't feel awkward and inexperienced. She felt beautiful, desirable and reckless.

With a laugh, Rebecca dipped under the surface to let the water, and the freedom, surround her. Who would have believed it?

"Does it always take so little to make you laugh?"

Rebecca ran a hand over her slicked-back hair. Stephen was treading water beside her, smoothly, hardly making a ripple. His skin was dark gold, glistening-wet. His hair was streaked by the sun and dampened by the water, which was almost exactly the color of his eyes. She had to suppress an urge to just reach out and touch.

"A secluded inlet, a beautiful sky, an interesting man." With another sigh, she kicked her legs up so that she could float. "It doesn't seem like so little to me." She studied the vague outline of the mountains, far out of reach. "I promised myself that no matter where I went, what I did, I'd never take anything for granted again."

There was something in the way she said it, some hint of sadness, that pulled at him. The urge to comfort wasn't completely foreign in him, but he hadn't had much practice at it. "Was there a man who hurt you?"

Her lips curved at that, but he couldn't know that she was laughing at herself. Naturally, she'd dated. They had been polite, cautious evenings, usually with little interest on either side. She'd been dull, or at least she had never worked up the nerve to spread her wings. Once or twice, when she'd felt a tug, she'd been too shy, too much the efficient Rebecca Malone, to do anything about it.

With him, everything was different. Because she loved him. She didn't know how, she didn't know why, but she loved him as much as any woman could love any man.

"No. There's no one." She closed her eyes, trusting the water to carry her. "When my parents died, it hurt. It hurt so badly that I suppose I pulled back from life. I thought it was important that I be a responsible adult, even though I wasn't nearly an adult yet."

Strange that she hadn't thought of it quite that way until she'd stopped being obsessively responsible. Stranger still was how easy it was to tell him what she'd never even acknowledged herself.

"My aunt Jeannie was kind and considerate and loving, but she'd forgotten what it was like to be a young girl. Suddenly I realized I'd missed being young, lazy, foolish, all the things everyone's entitled to be at least once. I decided to make up for it."

Her hair was spread out and drifting on the water.

Her eyes were closed, and her face was sheened with water. Not beautiful, Stephen told himself. She was too angular for real beauty. But she was fascinating…in looks, in philosophy…more, in the open-armed way she embraced whatever crossed her path.

He found himself looking around the inlet as he hadn't bothered to look at anything in years. He could see the sun dancing on the surface, could see the ripples spreading and growing from the quiet motion of their bodies. Farther away was the narrow curving strip of white beach, deserted now, but for a few birds fluttering over the sand. It was quiet, almost unnaturally quiet, the only sound the soft, monotonous slap of water against sand. And he was relaxed, totally, mind and body. Perhaps he, too, had forgotten what it was like to be young and foolish.

On impulse he put a hand on her shoulder and pushed her under.

She came up sputtering, dragging wet hair out of her eyes. He grinned at her and calmly continued to tread water. "It was too easy."

She tilted her head, considering him and the distance between them. Challenge leaped into her eyes, sparked with amusement. "It won't be the next time."

His grin only widened. When he moved, he moved fast, streaking under and across the water like an eel. Rebecca had time for a quick squeal. Dragging in a deep breath, she kicked out. He caught her ankle, but she was ready. Unresisting, she let him pull her under. Then, instead of fighting her way back to the surface, she wrapped her arms around him and sent them both rolling in an underwater wrestling match. They were still tangled, her arms around him, her hands hooked over his shoulders, when they surfaced.

"We're even." She gasped for air and shook the water out of her eyes.

"How do you figure?"

"If we'd had a mat I'd have pinned you. Want to go for two out of three?"

"I might." He felt her legs tangle with his as she kicked out lazily. "But for now I prefer this."

He was going to kiss her again. She saw it in his eyes, felt it in the slight tensing of the arm that locked them torso to torso. She wasn't sure she was ready. More, she was afraid she was much too ready.

"Stephen?"

"Hmm?" His lips were a breath away from hers. Then he found himself underwater again, his arms empty. He should have been furious. He nearly was when he pushed to surface. She was shoulder-deep in the water, a few feet away. Her laughter rolled over him, young, delighted, unapologetic.

"It was too easy." She managed a startled "whoops" when he struck out after her. She might have made it—

she had enough of a lead—but he swam as though he'd been born in the water. Still, she was agile, and she almost managed to dodge him, but her laughter betrayed her. She gulped in water, choked, then found herself hauled up into his arms in thigh-deep water.

"I like to win." Deciding it was useless to struggle, she pressed a hand to her heart and gasped for air. "It's a personality flaw. Sometimes I cheat at canasta."

"Canasta?" The last thing he could picture the slim, sexy bundle in his arms doing was spending a quiet evening playing cards.

"I can't help myself." Still breathless, she laid her head on his shoulder. "No willpower."

"I find myself having the same problem." With a careless toss, he sent her flying through the air. She hit the water bottom first.

"I guess I deserved that." She struggled to her feet, water raining off her. "I have to sit." Wading through the water, she headed for the gentle slope of beach. She lay, half in and half out of the water, not caring that the sand would cling to her hair and skin. When he dropped down beside her, she reached out a hand for his. "I don't know when I've had a nicer day."

He looked down to where her fingers linked with his. The gesture had been so easy, so natural. He wondered how it could both comfort and arouse. "It's hardly over."

"It seems like it could last forever." She wanted it to

go on and on. Blue skies and easy laughter. Cool water and endless hours. There had been a time, not so long before, when the days had dragged into nights and the nights into days. "Did you ever want to run away?"

With her hand still in his, he lay back to watch a few scattered rags of clouds drift. How long had it been, he wondered, since he'd really watched the sky? "To where?"

"Anywhere. Away from the way things are, away from what you're afraid they'll always be." She closed her eyes and could see herself brewing that first cup of coffee at exactly 7:15, opening the first file at precisely 9:01. "To drop out of sight," she murmured, "and pop up somewhere else, anywhere else, as someone completely different."

"You can't change who you are."

"Oh, but you can." Her tone suddenly urgent, she rose on her elbow. "Sometimes you have to."

He reached up to touch the ends of her hair. "What are you running from?"

"Everything. I'm a coward."

He looked into her eyes. They were so clear, so full of enthusiasm. "I don't think so."

"But you don't know me." A flicker of regret, then uncertainty, ran across her face. "I'm not sure I want you to."

"Don't I?" His fingers tightened on her hair, keeping her still. "There are people and circumstances that don't take months or years before they're understood. I look at you and something fits into place, Rebecca. I don't know why, but it is. I know you." He tugged her down for the lightest, the briefest, of kisses. "And I like what I see."

"Do you?" She smiled. "Really?"

"Do you imagine I spend the day with a woman only because I want to sleep with her?" She shrugged, and though her blush was very faint, he noticed it and was amused by it. How many women, he wondered, could kiss a man into oblivion, then blush? "Being with you, Rebecca, is a difficult pleasure."

She chuckled and began to draw circles in the wet sand. What would he say, what would he think, if he knew what she was? Or, more accurately, what she wasn't? It didn't matter, she told herself. She couldn't let it spoil what there was between them.

"I think that's the most wonderful compliment I've ever had."

"Where have you been?" he murmured.

When she moved restlessly, he held her still. "Don't. I'm not going to touch you. Not yet."

"That's not the problem." With her eyes closed, she tilted her chin up and let the sun beat down on her face. "The problem is, I want you to touch me, so much it frightens me." Taking her time, she sat up, gathering her courage. She wanted to be honest, and she hoped she wouldn't sound like a fool. "Stephen, I don't sleep around. I need you to understand, because this is all happening so quickly. But it's not casual."

He lifted a hand to her chin and turned her to face him. His eyes were as blue as the water, and, to her, as unfathomable. "No, it's not." He made the decision quickly, though he had been turning the idea over in his mind all day. "I have to go to Athens tomorrow. Come with me, Rebecca."

"Athens?" she managed, staring at him.

"Business. A day, two at the most. I'd like you with me." And he was afraid, more than he cared to admit, that when he returned she might be gone.

"I…" What should she say? What was right?

"You told me you'd planned to go." He'd push if necessary. Now that the idea had taken root, Stephen had no intention of going anywhere without her.

"Yes, but I wouldn't want to be in the way while you're working."

"You'll be in my way whether you're here or there."

Her head came up at that, and the look she gave him was both shy and stunning. He stifled the need to take her again, to roll until she was beneath him on the sand. He'd said he'd give her time. Perhaps what he'd really meant was that he needed time himself.

"You'll have your own suite. No strings, Rebecca. Just your company."

"A day or two," she murmured.

"It's a simple matter to have your room held for you here for your return."

Her return. Not his. If he left Corfu tomorrow she would probably never see him again. He was offering her another day, perhaps two. Never take anything for granted, she remembered. Never again.

Athens, she thought. It was true that she had planned to see it before she left Greece. But she would have gone alone. A few days before, that had been what she thought she wanted. The adventure of seeing new places, new people, on her own. Now the thought of going with him, of having him beside her when she first caught sight of the Acropolis, of having him want her with him, changed everything.

"I'd love to go with you." She rose quickly and dived into the water. She was in over her head.

CHAPTER 6

Athens was neither East nor West. It was spitted meat and spices roasting. It was tall buildings and modern shops. It was narrow, unpaved streets and clamorous bazaars. It had been the scene of revolution and brutality. It was ancient and civilized and passionate.

Rebecca quite simply fell in love at first sight.

She'd been seduced by Paris and charmed by London, but in Athens she lost her heart. She wanted to see everything at once, from sunrise to moonlight, and the heat-drenched afternoon between.

All that first morning, while Stephen was immersed in business meetings, she wandered. The hotel he'd chosen was lovely, but she was drawn to the streets and the people. Somehow she didn't feel like a visitor here. She felt like someone who had returned home after a long, long journey. Athens was waiting for her, ready to welcome her back.

Incredible. All her life she had accepted the parameters set for her. Now she was touring Old Athens, with its clicking worry beads and its open-fronted shops, where she could buy cheap plaster copies of monuments or elegant antiques.

She passed tavernas, but she was too excited to be tempted by the rich smells of coffee and baking. She heard the clear notes of a flute as she looked up and saw the Acropolis.

There was only one approach. Though it was still early, other tourists were making their way toward the ruins in twos and in groups. Rebecca let her camera hang by its strap. Despite the chattering around her, she felt alone, but beautifully so.

She would never be able to explain what it felt like to stand in the morning sun and look at something that had been built for the gods—something that had endured war and weather and time. It had been a place of worship. Even now, after centuries had passed, Rebecca felt the spiritual pull. Perhaps the goddess Athena, with her gleaming helmet and spear, still visited there.

Rebecca had been disappointed that Stephen couldn't join her on her first morning in Athens. Now she was glad to be alone—to sit and absorb and imagine without having to explain her thoughts.

How could she, after having seen so much, go back to so little? Sighing, she wandered through the temples. It wasn't just the awe she felt here, or the excitement she had felt in London and Paris, that had changed her. It was Stephen and everything she'd felt, everything she'd wanted, since she'd met him.

Perhaps she would go back to Philadelphia, but she would never be the same person. Once you fell in love, completely, totally in love, nothing was ever the same.

She wished it could be simple, the way she imagined it was simple for so many other women. An attractive man, a physical tug. But with Stephen, as with Athens, she'd lost her heart. However implausible it seemed, she had recognized the man, as well as the city, as being part of her, as being for her. Desire, when tangled up with love, could never be simple.

But how could you be sure you were in love when it had never happened to you before? If she were home, at least she would have a friend to talk to. With a little laugh, Rebecca walked out into the sunlight. How many times had she been on the receiving end of a long, scattered conversation from a friend who had fallen in love—or thought she had. The excitement, the unhappiness, the thrills. Sometimes she'd been envious, and sometimes she'd been grateful not to have the complication in her own life. But always, always, she'd offered calm, practical, even soothing advice.

Oddly enough, she didn't seem to be able to do the same for herself.

All she could think of was the way her heart pounded when he touched her, how excitement, panic and anticipation fluttered through her every time he looked at her. When she was with him, her feelings and fantasies seemed reasonable. When she was with him, she could believe in fate, in the matching of soul to soul.

It wasn't enough. At least that was what she would have told another woman. Attraction and passion weren't enough. Yet there was no explaining, even to herself, the sense of rightness she experienced whenever she was with him. If she were a fanciful person she would say it was as though she'd been waiting for him, waiting for the time and the place for him to come to her.

It sounded simple—if fate could be considered simple. Yet beneath all the pleasure and that sense of reunion was guilt. She couldn't shake it, and she knew she wouldn't be able to ignore it much longer. She wasn't the woman she had let him believe her to be. She wasn't the well-traveled at-loose-ends free spirit she pretended to be. No matter how many ties she'd cut, she was still Rebecca Malone. How would he feel about her once he knew how limited and dull her life had been?

How and when was she going to tell him?

A few more days, she promised herself as she began

the walk back. It was selfish, perhaps it was even dangerous, but she wanted just a few more days.

It was midafternoon before she returned to the hotel. Ignoring the fact that she might be considered overeager, she went straight to Stephen's suite. She couldn't wait to see him, to tell him everything she'd seen, to show him everything she'd bought. Her easy smile faded a bit when his secretary Elana opened the door.

"Miss Malone." Gracious and self-confident, Elana waved her in. "Please sit down. I'll let Stephen know you're here."

"I don't want to interrupt." Rebecca shifted her bags, feeling gauche and foolish.

"Not at all. Have you just come in?"

"Yes, I…" For the first time, Rebecca noticed that her skin was damp and her hair tousled. In contrast, Elana was cool and perfectly groomed. "I really should go."

"Please." Elana urged Rebecca to a chair. "Let me get you a drink." With a half smile, Elana began to pour a tall glass of iced juice. She had expected Stephen's mystery lady to be smooth, controlled and stunning. It pleased her a great deal to find Rebecca wide-eyed, a little unsure, and clearly a great deal in love.

"Did you enjoy your morning?"

"Yes, very much." She accepted the glass and tried to relax. Jealousy, she realized, feeling herself flush at the

realization. She couldn't remember ever having experienced the sensation before. Who wouldn't be jeal-
ous? she asked herself as she watched Elana walk to the
phone. The Greek woman was gorgeous, self-con-
tained, coolly efficient. Above all, she had a relationship
with Stephen that Rebecca knew nothing about. How
long has she known him? Rebecca wondered. And
how well?

"Stephen's just finishing up some business," Elana
said as she hung up the phone. With easy, economical
moves, she poured herself a drink, then walked to the
chair facing Rebecca. "What do you think of Athens?"

"I love it." Rebecca wished she'd taken the time to
brush her hair and freshen her makeup. Lecturing herself, she sipped at her juice. "I'm not sure what I expected, but it's everything and more."

"Europeans see it as the East, Orientals see it as the
West." Elana crossed her legs and settled back. It surprised her to realize that she was prepared to like Rebecca Malone. "What Athens is is Greek—and, more
particularly, Athenian." She paused, studying Rebecca
over the rim of her glass. "People often view Stephen
in much the same way, and what he is is Stephen."

"How long have you worked for him?"

"Five years."

"You must know him well."

"Better than some. He's a demanding and generous

employer and an interesting man. Fortunately, I like to travel and I enjoy my work."

Rebecca rubbed at a spot of dust on her slacks. "It never occurred to me that farming required so much traveling. I never realized how much was involved in growing olives."

Elana's brows rose in obvious surprise, but she continued smoothly when Rebecca glanced back at her. "Whatever Stephen does, he does thoroughly." She smiled to herself, satisfied. She hadn't been certain until now whether the American woman was attracted to Stephen or to his position. "Has Stephen explained to you about the dinner party this evening?"

"He said something about a small party here at the hotel. A business dinner."

"Men take these things more lightly than women." Feeling friendlier, Elena offered her first genuine smile. "It will be small, but quite extravagant." She watched as Rebecca automatically lifted a hand to her hair. "If you need anything—a dress, a salon—the hotel can accommodate you."

Rebecca thought of the casual sportswear she'd tossed into her bag before the impulsive trip to Athens. "I need everything."

With a quick, understanding laugh, Elana rose. "I'll make some calls for you."

"Thank you, but I don't want to interfere with your work."

"Seeing that you're comfortable is part of my work." They both glanced over when the door opened. "Stephen. You see, she hasn't run away." Taking her glass and her pad, she left them alone.

"You were gone a long time." He hated the fact that he'd begun to watch the clock and worry. He'd imagined her hurt or abducted. He'd begun to wonder if she would disappear from his life as quickly as she'd appeared in it. Now she was here, her eyes alive with pleasure, her clothes rumpled and her hair windblown.

"I guess I got caught up exploring." She started to rise, but before she could gain her feet he was pulling her out of the chair, seeking, finding her mouth with his.

His desperation whipped through her. His hunger incited her own. Without thought, without hesitation, she clung to him, answering, accepting. Already seduced, she murmured something, an incoherent sound that caught in her throat.

Good God, he thought, it wasn't possible, it wasn't sane, to want like this. Throughout the morning while all the facts and figures and demands of business had been hammering at him, he'd thought of her, of holding her, of tasting her, of being with her. When she had stayed away for so long he'd begun to imagine, then to fear, what his life would be like without her.

It wasn't going to happen. He scraped his teeth over her bottom lip, and she gasped and opened for him. He wouldn't let it happen. Where she came from, where she intended to go, no longer mattered. She belonged to him now. And, though he'd only begun to deal with it, he belonged to her.

But he needed some sanity, some logic. Fighting himself, Stephen drew her away from him. Her eyes remained closed, and her lips remained parted. A soft, sultry sound escaped them as her lashes fluttered upward.

"I..." She took a deep breath and let it out slowly. "I should go sightseeing more often."

Gradually he realized how hard his fingers were pressing into her arms. As if he were afraid she would slip away. Cursing himself, he relaxed. "I would have preferred to go with you."

"I understand you're busy. I'd have bored you silly, poking into every shop and staring at every column."

"No." If there was one thing he was certain of, it was that she would never bore him. "I'd like to have seen your first impression of Athens."

"It was like coming home," she told him, then hurried on because it sounded foolish. "I couldn't get enough." Laughing at herself, she gestured toward her bags. "Obviously. It's so different from anywhere I've ever been. At the Acropolis I couldn't even take any pictures, because I knew they couldn't capture the feeling. Then I walked along the streets and saw old men with *kom—konbou—*" She fumbled over the Greek and finally made a helpless gesture.

"Kombouloi," he murmured. "Worry beads."

"Yes, and I imagined how they might sit in those shadowy doorways watching the tourists go by, day after day, year after year." She sat, pleased to share her impressions with him. "I saw a shop with all these costumes, lots of tinsel, and some really dreadful plaster copies of the monuments."

He grinned and sat beside her. "How many did you buy?"

"Three or four." She bent down to rattle through her bags. "I bought you a present."

"A plaster statue of Athena?"

She glanced up, eyes laughing. "Almost. Then I found this tiny antique shop in the old section. It was all dim and dusty and irresistible. The owner had a handful of English phrases, and I had my phrase book. After we'd confused each other completely, I bought this."

She drew out an S-shaped porcelain pipe decorated with paintings of the wild mountain goats of Greece. Attached to it was a long wooden stem, as smooth as glass, tipped by a tarnished brass mouthpiece.

"I remembered the goats we'd seen on Corfu," she explained as Stephen examined it. "I thought you might like it, though I've never seen you smoke a pipe."

With a quiet laugh, he looked back at her, balancing the gift in both hands. "No, I don't—at least not of this nature."

"Well, it's more ornamental than functional, I suppose. The man couldn't tell me much about it—at least not that I could understand." She reached out to run a finger along the edge of the bowl. "I've never seen anything like it."

"I'm relieved to hear it." When she sent him a puzzled look, he leaned over to brush her lips with his. "*Matia mou,* this is a hashish pipe."

"A hashish pipe?" She stared, first in shock, then in fascination. "Really? I mean, did people actually use it?"

"Undoubtedly. Quite a number, I'd say, since it's at least a hundred and fifty years old."

"Imagine that." She pouted, imagining dark, smoky dens. "I guess it's not a very appropriate souvenir."

"On the contrary, whenever I see it I'll think of you."

She glanced up quickly, unsure, but the amusement in his eyes had her smiling again. "I should have bought you the plaster statue of Athena."

Taking her hands, he drew her to her feet. "I'm flattered that you bought me anything." She felt the subtle change as his fingers tightened on hers. "I want time with you, Rebecca. Hours of it. Days. There's too much I need to know." When she lowered her gaze, he caught her chin. "What are those secrets of yours?"

"Nothing that would interest you."

"You're wrong. Tomorrow I intend to find out all there is to know." He saw the quick flicker of unease in her eyes. Other men, he thought with an uncomfortable surge of jealousy. The hell with them. "No more evasions. I want you, all of you. Do you understand?"

"Yes, but—"

"Tomorrow." He cut her off, suddenly, completely, frustratingly Greek. "I have business that can't be avoided now. I'll come for you at seven."

"All right."

Tomorrow was years away, she told herself. She had time to decide what she would say, how she would say it. Before tomorrow came tonight. She would be everything she'd ever wanted to be, everything he wanted her to be.

"I'd better go." Before he could touch her again, she bent to gather her bags. "Stephen…" She paused at the door and turned to look at him as he stood in the middle of the room, comfortable with the wealth that surrounded him, confident with who and what he was. "You might be disappointed when you find out."

She left quickly, leaving him frowning after her.

CHAPTER 7

She was as nervous as a cat. Every time she looked in the mirror Rebecca wondered who the woman was who was staring back at her. It wasn't a stranger, but it was a very, very different Rebecca Malone.

Was it just the different hairstyle, poufed and frizzed and swept around her face? Could it be the dress, the glittery spill of aquamarine that left her arms and shoulders bare? No, it was more than that. More than makeup and clever stylists and glamorous clothes. It was in her eyes. How could she help but see it? How could anyone? The woman who looked back from the mirror was a woman in love.

What was she going to do about it? What could she do? she asked herself. She was still practical enough to accept that some things could never be changed. But was she bold enough, or strong enough, to take what she wanted and live with the consequences?

When she heard the knock on the door, Rebecca took a deep breath and picked up the useless compact-size evening bag she'd bought just that afternoon. It was all happening so fast. When she'd come back from Stephen's suite there had been a detailed message from Elana listing appointments—for a massage, a facial, hair-styling—along with the name of the manager of the hotel's most exclusive boutique. She hadn't had time to think, even for a minute, about her evening with Stephen. Or about any tomorrows.

Perhaps that was best, she decided as she pulled open the door. It was best not to think, not to analyze. It was best to accept and to act.

She looked like a siren, some disciple of Circe, with her windswept hair and a dress the color of seductive seas. Had he told himself she wasn't beautiful? Had he believed it? At that moment he was certain he'd never seen, never would see, a more exciting woman.

"You're amazing, Rebecca." He took her hand and drew her to him so that they stood in the doorway to-gether. On the threshold.

"Why? Because I'm on time?"

"Because you're never what I expect." He brought her hand to his lips. "And always what I want."

Because she was speechless, she was glad when he

closed the door at her back and led her to the eleva-
tors. He looked different from the man she had first met,
the one who dressed with such casual elegance. Tonight
there was a formality about him, and the sophistication
she had sensed earlier was abundantly apparent in the
ease with which he wore the black dinner jacket.

"The way you look," he told her, "it seems a shame
to waste the evening on a business dinner."

"I'm looking forward to meeting some of your
friends."

"Associates," he said with an odd smile. "When you've
been poor—and don't intend to be poor again—you
rarely make friends in business."

She frowned. This was a side of him, the business
side, that she didn't know. Would he be ruthless? She
looked at him, saw it, and accepted it. Yes, a man like
Stephen would always be ruthless with what belonged
to him. "But enemies?"

"The same rule, in business, applies to friends and enemies. My father taught me more than fishing, Rebecca.
He also taught me that to succeed, to attain, you must
learn not only how to trust, but how far."

"I've never been poor, but I imagine it's frightening."

"Strengthening." He took her hand again when the
elevator doors opened. "We have different backgrounds,
Rebecca, but, fortunately, we've come to the same
place."

He had no idea *how* different. Trust. He had spoken of trust. She discovered she wanted to tell him, tell him everything. Tell him that she knew nothing of elegant parties and glamorous life-styles. She was a fraud, and when he found out he might laugh at her and brush her aside. But she wanted him to know.

"Stephen, I want to—"

"Stephen. Once more you outdo us all in your choice of women."

"Dimitri."

Rebecca stopped, caught on the brink of confession. The man who faced her was classically handsome. His silver mane contrasted with bronzed skin lined by a half century of sun. He wore a mustache that swept majestically over gleaming teeth.

"It was kind of you to invite us here this evening, but it would be kinder still to introduce me to your lovely companion."

"Rebecca Malone, Dimitri Petropolis."

A diamond glittered on the hand he lifted to clasp Rebecca's. The hand itself was hard as rock. "A pleasure. Athens is already abuzz with talk of the woman who arrived with Stephen."

Certain he was joking, she smiled. "Then Athens must be in desperate need of news."

His eyes widened for a moment, then creased at the

corners when he laughed. "I have no doubt you will provide an abundance of it."

Stephen slipped a hand under Rebecca's elbow. The look he sent Dimitri was very quick and very clear. They had competed over land, but there would be no competition over Rebecca.

"If you'll excuse us a moment, Dimitri, I'd like to get Rebecca some champagne."

"Of course." Amused—and challenged—Dimitri brushed at his mustache as he watched them walk away.

Rebecca had no way of knowing that to Stephen a small dinner party meant a hundred people. She sipped her first glass of wine, hoping she wouldn't embarrass them both by being foolishly shy and tongue-tied. In the past, whenever she had found herself in a crowd, she had always looked for the nearest corner to fade into. Not tonight, she promised herself, straightening her shoulders.

There were dozens of names to remember, but she filed them away as easily as she had always filed numbers. In the hour before dinner, while the guests mixed and mingled, she found herself at ease. The stomach flutters and hot blushes she'd often experienced at parties and functions simply didn't happen.

Perhaps she was the new Rebecca Malone after all.

She heard business discussed here and there. Most of it seemed to be hotel and resort business—talk of remodeling and expansions, mergers and takeovers. She found it odd that so many of the guests were in that trade, rather than prosperous farmers or olive growers.

Stephen came up behind her and murmured in her ear, "You look pleased with yourself."

"I am." He couldn't know that she was pleased to find herself at ease and comfortable in a party of strangers. "So many interesting people."

"Interesting." He brushed a finger over her wispy bangs. "I thought you might find it dull."

"Not at all." She took a last sip of champagne, then set the glass aside. Instantly a waiter was at her side, offering another. Stephen watched her smile her thanks.

"So you enjoy parties?"

"Sometimes. I'm enjoying this one, and having a chance to meet your associates."

Stephen glanced over her shoulder, summing up the looks and quiet murmurs. "They'll be talking about you for weeks to come."

She only laughed, turning in a slow circle. Around her was the flash of jewels and the gleam of gold. The sleek and the prosperous, the rich and the successful. It pleased her that she'd found more to talk about than tax shelters.

"I can't imagine they have so little on their minds. This is such a gorgeous room."

She looked around the huge ballroom, with its

cream-and-rose walls, its glittering chandeliers and its gleaming floors. There were alcoves for cozy love seats and tall, thriving ornamental trees in huge copper pots. The tables, arranged to give a sense of intimacy, were already set with ivory cloths and slender tapers.

"It's really a beautiful hotel," she continued. "Everything about it runs so smoothly." She smiled up at him. "I'm torn between the resort in Corfu and this."

"Thank you." When she gave him a blank look, he tipped up her chin with his finger. "They're mine."

"Your what?"

"My hotels," he said simply, then led her to a table.

She spoke all through dinner, though for the first fifteen minutes she had no idea what she said. There were eight at Stephen's table, including Dimitri, who had shifted name cards so that he could sit beside her. She toyed with her seafood appetizer, chatted and wondered if she could have made a bigger fool out of herself.

He wasn't simply prosperous. He wasn't simply well-off. There was enough accountant left in Rebecca to understand that when a man owned what Stephen owned he was far, far more than comfortable.

What would he think of her when he found out what she was? Trust? How could she ever expect him to trust her now? She swallowed without tasting and

managed to smile. Would he think she was a gold dig-
ger, that she had set herself up to run into him?

No, that was ridiculous.

She forced herself to look over and saw that Stephen
was watching her steadily. She picked up her fork with
one hand and balled up the napkin in her lap with the
other.

Why couldn't he be ordinary? she wondered. Someone vacationing, someone working at the resort? Why had
she fallen in love with someone so far out of her reach?

"Have you left us?"

Rebecca jerked herself back to see Dimitri smiling
at her. Flushing, she noticed that the next course had
been served while she'd been daydreaming. "I'm sorry."
With an effort she began to toy with the *salata Athenas*.

"A beautiful woman need never apologize for being
lost in her own thoughts." He patted her hand, then let
his fingers linger. He caught Stephen's dark look and
smiled. If he didn't like the boy so much, he thought,
he wouldn't get nearly so much pleasure from irritat-
ing him. "Tell me, how did you meet Stephen?"

"We met in Corfu." She thought of that first meal
they had shared…quiet, relaxed, alone.

"Ah, soft nights and sunny days. You are vacationing?"

"Yes." Rebecca put more effort into her smile. If she
stared into her salad she would only embarrass herself,
and Stephen. "He was kind enough to show me some
of the island."

"He knows it well, and many of the other islands of our country. There's something of the gypsy in him."

She had sensed that. Hadn't that been part of the attraction? Hadn't Rebecca just discovered the gypsy in herself? "Have you know him long?"

"We have a long-standing business relationship. Friendly rivals, you might say. When Stephen was hardly more than a boy he accumulated an impressive amount of land." He gestured expansively. "As you can see, he used it wisely. I believe he has two hotels in your country."

"Two? More?" Rebecca picked up her glass and took a long swallow of wine.

"So you see, I had wondered if you had met in America and were old friends."

"No." Rebecca nodded weakly as the waiter removed the salad and replaced it with moussaka. "We only just met a few days ago."

"As always, Stephen moves quickly and stylishly." Dimitri took her hand again, more than a little amused by the frown he saw deepening in Stephen's eyes. "Where is it in America you are from?"

"Philadelphia." Relax, she ordered herself. Relax and enjoy. "That's in the Northeast."

It infuriated Stephen to watch her flirting so easily, so effectively, with another man. She sat through course after course, barely eating, all the while gifting Dimitri with her shy smiles. Not once did she draw away when the older man touched her hand or leaned close. From where he sat, Stephen could catch a trace of her scent, soft, subtle, maddening. He could hear her quiet laugh when Dimitri murmured something in her ear.

Then she was standing with him, her hand caught in his, as he led her to the dance floor.

Stephen sat there, battling back a jealousy he despised, and watched them move together to music made for lovers. Under the lights her dress clung, then swayed, then shifted. Her face was close, too damn close, to Dimitri's. He knew what it was like to hold her like that, to breathe in the scent of her skin and her hair. He knew what it was to feel her body brush against his, to feel the life, the passion, bubbling. He knew what it was to see her eyes blur, her lips part, to hear that quiet sigh.

He had often put his stamp on land, but never on a woman. He didn't believe in it. But only a fool sat idly by and allowed another man to enjoy what was his. With a muttered oath, Stephen rose, strode out onto the dance floor and laid a hand on Dimitri's shoulder.

"Ah, well." The older man gave a regretful sigh and stepped aside. "Until later."

Before she could respond, Rebecca was caught against Stephen. With a sigh of her own, she relaxed and matched her steps to his. Maybe it was like a dream, she told herself as she closed her eyes and let the music fill her head. But she was going to enjoy every moment until it was time to wake up.

She seemed to melt against him. Her fingers moved lightly through his hair as she rested her cheek against his. Was this the way she'd danced with Dimitri? Stephen wondered, then cursed himself. He was being a fool, but he couldn't seem to stop himself. Then again, he'd had to fight for everything else in his life. Why should his woman be any different?

He wanted to drag her off then and there, away from everyone, and find some dark, quiet place to love her.

"You're enjoying yourself?"

"Yes." She wouldn't think about what he was, not now. Soon enough the night would be over and tomorrow would have to be faced. While the music played and he held her, she would only think of what he meant to her. "Very much."

The dreamy tone of her voice almost undid him. "Apparently Dimitri entertained you well."

"Mmm. He's a very nice man."

"You moved easily from his arms to mine."

Something in his tone pried through the pleasure she felt. Carefully she drew back so that she could see his face. "I don't think I know what you mean."

"I believe you do."

She was tempted to laugh, but there was no humor in Stephen's eyes. Rebecca felt her stomach knot as it always did when she was faced with a confrontation. "If I do, then I'd have to think you ridiculous. Maybe we'd better go back to the table."

"So you can be with him?" Even as the words came out he realized the unfairness, even the foolishness, of them.

She stiffened, retreating as far as she could from anger. "I don't think this is the place for this kind of discussion."

"You're quite right." As furious with himself as he was with her, he pulled her from the dance floor.

CHAPTER 8

꧁

"Stop it." By the time he'd dragged her to the eleva-
tors, Rebecca had gotten over her first shock. "What's
gotten into you?"

"I'm simply taking you to a more suitable place for
our discussion." He pulled her into the elevator, then
punched the button for their floor.

"You have guests," she began, but he sent her a look
than made her feel like a fool. Falling back on dignity,
she straightened her shoulders. "I prefer to be asked if
I want to leave, not dragged around as though I were a
pack mule."

Though her heart was pounding, she sailed past him
when the doors opened, intending to breeze into her
own rooms and slam the door in his face. In two steps
he had her arm again. Rebecca found herself guided,
none too gently, into Stephen's suite.

"I don't want to talk to you," she said, because she was certain her teeth would begin to chatter at any moment. She didn't argue well in the best of circumstances. Faced with Stephen's anger, she was certain she would lose.

He said nothing as he loosened his tie and the first two buttons of his shirt. He went to the bar and poured two brandies. He was being irrational and he knew it, but he seemed unable to control it. That was new, he decided. But there had been many new emotions in him since Rebecca.

Walking back to Rebecca, he set one snifter by her elbow. When he looked at her…he wanted to shout, to beg, to demand, to plead. As a result, his voice was clipped and hard.

"You came to Athens with me, not with Dimitri or any other man."

She didn't touch the snifter. She was certain her hands would shake so hard that it would slip out of her grip. "Is that a Greek custom?" It amazed her—and bolstered her confidence—to hear how calm her voice was. "Forbidding a woman to speak to another man?"

"Speak?" He could still see the way Dimitri had bent his head close to hers. Dimitri, who was smooth and practiced. Dimitri, whose background would very likely mirror Rebecca's. Old money, privileged childhoods, quiet society. "Do you allow every man who speaks to you to hold you, to touch you?"

She didn't blush. Instead, the color faded from her cheeks. She shook, not with fear but with fury. "What I do, and with whom I do it, is my business. Mine."

Very deliberately he lifted his snifter and drank. "No."

"If you think that because I came here with you, you have the right to dictate to me you're wrong. I'm my own person, Stephen." It struck her even as she said it that it was true. She was her own person. Each decision she made was her own. Filled with a new sense of power, she stepped forward. "No one owns me, not you, not anyone. I won't be ordered, I won't be forced, I won't be pressured." With a flick of her skirts, she turned. He had her again quickly, his hands on both of her arms, his face close.

"You won't go back to him."

"You couldn't stop me if that was what I wanted." She tossed her head back challengingly. "But I have no intention of going back downstairs to Dimitri, or anyone else." She jerked her arms free. "You idiot. Why should I want to be with him when I'm in love with you?"

She stopped, her eyes wide with shock, her lips parted in surprise. Overwhelmed by a combination of humiliation and fury, she spun around. Then she was struggling against him. "Leave me alone! Oh, God, just leave me alone!"

"Do you think I could let you go now?" He caught her hair in his hand, dragging it back until her eyes met his. In them she saw triumph and desire. "I feel as though I've waited all my life to hear you say those words." He rained kisses over her face until her struggles ceased. "You drive me mad," he murmured. "Being with you, being without you."

"Please." Colors, shapes, lights were whirling in her head. "I need to think."

"No. Ask me for anything else, but not more time." Gathering her close, he buried his face in her hair. "Do you think I make a fool of myself over every woman?"

"I don't know." She moaned when his lips trailed down her throat. Something wild and terrifying was happening inside her body. "I don't know you. You don't know me."

"Yes, I do." He pulled away just far enough to look down at her. "From the first moment I saw you, I knew you. Needed you. Wanted you."

It was true. She knew it, felt it, but she shook her head in denial. "It's not possible."

"I've loved you before, Rebecca, almost as much as I do now." He felt her go still. The color fled from her face again, but her eyes stayed steady on his.

"I don't want you to say what isn't real, what you're not sure of."

"Didn't you feel it, the first time I kissed you?" When he saw the acknowledgment in her eyes, his grip tightened. He could feel her heart thundering, racing to match the rhythm of his own. "Somehow you've come back to me, and I to you. No more questions," he said, before she could speak. "I need you tonight."

It was real. She felt the truth and the knowledge when his mouth found hers. If it was wrong to go blindly into need, then she would pay whatever price was asked. She could no longer deny him...or herself.

There was no gentleness in the embrace. It was as it had been the first time, lovers reunited, a hunger finally quenched. All heat and light. She gave more than she'd known she had. Her mouth was as avid as his, as seeking. Her murmurs were as desperate. Her hands didn't shake as they moved over him. They pressed, gripped, demanded. Greedy, she tugged the jacket from his shoulders.

Yes, he'd come back to her. If it was madness to believe it, then for tonight she'd be mad.

The taste of her, just the taste of her, was making his head swim and his blood boil. He nipped at her lip, then sucked until he heard her helpless whimper. He wanted her helpless. Something fierce and uncivilized inside him wanted her weak and pliant and defenseless. When she went limp in his arms he dived into her mouth and plundered. Her response tore at him, so sweet, so vulnerable, then suddenly so ardent.

Her hands, which had fluttered helplessly to her side, rose up again to pull at his shirt, to race under it to warmed flesh. She could only think of how right it felt to touch him, to press against him and wait for him to light new fires inside her.

With an oath, he swept her up into his arms and carried her to the bedroom.

The moon was waning and offered only the most delicate light. It fell in slants and shadows on the bed, dreamlike. But the vibrating of Rebecca's pulse told her this was no dream. There was the scent of jasmine from the sprigs in the vase beside the bed. It was a scent she would always remember, just as she would remember how dark and deep were the color of his eyes.

Needful, desperate, they tumbled onto the bed.

He wanted to take care with her. She seemed so small, so fragile. He wanted to show her how completely she filled his heart. But his body was on fire, and she was already moving like a whirlwind beneath him.

His mouth was everywhere, making her shudder and arch and ache. Desires she'd never known sprang to life inside her and took control. Delirious, she obeyed them, reveled in them, then searched for more.

They rolled across the bed in a passionate war that would have two victors, touching, taking, discovering. Impatient, he peeled the dress from her, moaning as he found her breasts with his hands, his lips, his teeth. Unreasoning desire catapulted through him when he felt her soar.

Her body felt like a furnace, impossibly hot, impossibly strong. Sensations rammed into her, stealing her breath. Mindless and moaning, she writhed under him, open for any demand he might make, pulsing for any new knowledge he might offer.

Finally, finally, she knew what it was to love, to be loved, to be wanted beyond reason. Naked, she clung to him, awash in the power and the weakness, the glory and the terror.

He raced over her as if he already knew what would make her tremble, what would make her yearn. Never before had she been so aware, so in tune with another.

She made him feel like a god. He touched, and her skin vibrated under his hand. He tasted, and her flavor was like no other. She was moist, heated, and utterly willing. She seemed to explode beneath him, lost in pleasure, drugged by passion. No other woman had ever driven him so close to madness. Her head was thrown back, and one hand was flung out as her fingers dug into the sheets. Wanton, waiting, wild.

With her name on his lips, he drove into her. His breath caught. His mind spun. Her cry of pain and release echoed in his head, bringing him both triumph and guilt. His body went rigid as he fought to claw his way back. Then she seemed to close around him, body, heart, soul. As helpless as she, he crossed the line into madness and took her with him.

CHAPTER 9

Aftershocks of passion wracked her. Stunned and confused, she lay in the shadowed light. Nothing had prepared her for this. No one had ever warned her that pleasure could be so huge or that need could be so jagged. If she had known… Rebecca closed her eyes and nearly laughed out loud. If she had known, she would have left everything behind years ago and searched the world for him.

Only him. She let out a quiet, calming sigh. Only him.

He was cursing himself, slowly, steadily, viciously. Innocent. Dear God. She'd been innocent, as fresh and untouched as spring, and he'd used her, hurt her, taken her.

Disgusted with himself, he sat up and reached for a cigar. He needed more than tobacco. He needed a drink, but he didn't trust his legs to carry him.

The flick of his lighter sounded like a gunshot. For

an instant his face, hardened by anger and self-loathing, was illuminated.

"Why didn't you tell me?"

Still floating on an ocean of pleasure, she blinked her eyes open. "What?"

"Damn it, Rebecca, why didn't you tell me you hadn't been with a man before? That this—that I was your first?"

There was an edge of accusation in his voice. For the first time, she realized she was naked. Her cheeks grew hot as she fumbled for the sheet. One moment there was glory; the next, shame. "I didn't think of it."

"Didn't think of it?" His head whipped around. "Don't you think I had a right to know? Do you think this would have happened if I had known?"

She shook her head. It was true that she hadn't thought of it. It hadn't mattered. He was the first, the last, the only. But now it occurred to her that a man like him might not want to make love with an inexperienced woman. "I'm sorry." Her heart seemed to shrivel in her breast. "You said that you loved me, that you wanted me. The rest didn't seem to matter."

She'd cried out. He'd heard the shock and pain in her voice. And he hadn't been able to stop himself. Yes, he needed a drink. "It mattered," he tossed back as he rose and strode into the other room.

Alone, she let out a shuddering breath. Of course it

mattered. Only a fool would have thought otherwise. He'd thought he was dealing with an experienced, emotionally mature woman who knew how to play the game. Words like *love* and *need* and *want* were interchangeable. Yes, he'd said he loved her, but to many love was physical and physical only.

She'd made a fool of herself and she'd infuriated him, and all because she'd begun a relationship built on illusions.

She'd knowingly taken the risk, Rebecca reminded herself as she climbed out of bed. Now she'd pay the price.

He was calmer when he started back to the bedroom. Calmer, though anger still bubbled inside him. First he would show her how it should have been, how it could be. Then they had to talk, rationally, coherently.

"Rebecca…" But when he looked at the bed it was empty.

She was wrapped in a robe and was hurling clothing into her suitcase when she heard him knock. With a shake of her head, she rubbed the tears from her cheeks and continued her frenzied packing. She wouldn't answer…. She wouldn't answer and be humiliated again.

"Rebecca." The moment of calm he'd achieved had vanished. Swearing through gritted teeth, he pounded on the door. "Rebecca, this is ridiculous. Open this door."

Ignoring him, she swept bottles and tubes of toiletries off the bureau and into her bag. He'd go away, she told herself, hardly aware that she'd begun to sob. He'd go away and then she'd leave, take a cab to the airport and catch the first plane to anywhere.

The sound of splintering wood had her rushing into the parlor in time to see the door give way.

She'd thought she'd seen fury before, but she'd been wrong. She saw it now as she stared into Stephen's face. Speechless, she looked from him to the broken door and back again.

Elana, tying the belt of her robe, rushed down the hall. "Stephen, what's happened? Is there a—"

He turned on her, hurling one short sentence in clipped Greek at her. Her eyes widened and she backed away, sending Rebecca a look that combined sympathy and envy.

"Do you think you have only to walk away from me?" He pushed the door back until it scraped against the battered jamb.

"I want—" Rebecca lifted a hand to her throat as if to push the words out. "I want to be alone."

"The hell with what you want." He started toward her, only to stop dead when she cringed and turned away. He'd forgotten what it was like to hurt, truly hurt, until that moment. "I asked you once if you were afraid of me. Now I see that you are." Searching for control, he dipped his hands into the pockets of the slacks he'd thrown on. She looked defenseless, terrified, and tears still streaked her cheeks. "I won't hurt you again. Will you sit?" When she shook her head, he bit off an oath. "I will."

"I know you're angry with me," she began when he'd settled into a chair. "I'll apologize if it'll do any good, but I do want to be alone."

His eyes had narrowed and focused. "You'll apologize? For what?"

"For…" What did he expect her to say? Humiliated, she crossed her arms and hugged her elbows. "For what happened…for not…explaining," she finished lamely. "For whatever you like," she continued as the tears started again. "Just leave me alone."

"Sweet God." He rubbed a weary hand over his face. "I can think of nothing in my life I've handled as badly as this." He rose, but stopped again when she automatically retreated. "You don't want me to touch you." His voice had roughened. He had to swallow to clear his throat. "I won't, but I hope you'll listen."

"There's nothing more to say. I understand how you feel and why you feel it. I'd rather we just left it at that."

"I treated you inexcusably."

"I don't want an apology."

"Rebecca—"

"I don't." Her voice rose, stopping his words, stopping her tears. "It's my fault. It's been my fault all along.

No, no, no!" she shouted when he took another step. "I don't want you to touch me. I couldn't bear it."

He sucked in his breath, then let it out slowly. "You twist the knife well."

But she was shaking her head and pacing the room now. "It didn't matter at first—at least I didn't think it would matter. I didn't know who you were or that I would fall in love with you. Now I've waited too long and ruined everything."

"What are you talking about?"

Perhaps it was best, best for both of them, to lay out the truth. "You said you knew me, but you don't, because I've done nothing but lie to you, right from the first moment."

Slowly, carefully, he lowered himself to the arm of a chair. "What have you lied to me about?"

"Everything." Her eyes were drenched with regret when she looked at him. "Then, tonight… First I found out that you own hotels. *Own* them."

"It was hardly a secret. Why should it matter?"

"It wouldn't." She dropped her hands to her sides. "If I was what I'd pretended to be. After we'd made love and you—I realized that by pretending I'd let you have feelings for someone who didn't even exist."

"You're standing in front of me, Rebecca. You exist."

"No. Not the way you think, not the way I've let you think."

He prepared himself for the worst. "What have you done? Were you running away from America?"

"No. Yes." She had to laugh at that. "Yes, I was running." She gathered what composure she had left and folded her hands. "I did come from Philadelphia, as I told you. I've lived there all my life. Lived there, went to school there, worked there." She found a tissue in the pocket of her robe. "I'm an accountant."

He stared at her, one brow lifting, as she blew her nose. "I beg your pardon?"

"I said, I'm an accountant." She hurled the words at him, then whirled away to face the window. Stephen started to rise, then thought better of it.

"I find it difficult to imagine you tallying ledgers, Rebecca. If you'd sit down, maybe we could talk this through."

"Damn it, I said I'm an accountant. A CPA, specializing in corporate taxes. Up until a few weeks ago I worked for McDowell, Jableki and Kline in Philadelphia."

He spread his hands, taking it all in. "All right. What did you do? Embezzle?"

She tossed back her head and nearly exploded with laughter. If she said yes he'd probably be intrigued. But the time for intrigue was over. The time for the truth was now. "No. I've never done anything illegal in my life. I've never even had a parking ticket. I've never done anything at all out of the ordinary until a few weeks ago."

She began to pace again, too agitated to keep still. "I'd never traveled, never had a man send a bottle of champagne to my table, never walked along the beach in the moonlight, never had a lover."

He said nothing, not because he was angry or bored but because he was fascinated.

"I had a good job, my car was paid for, I had good, conservative investments that would have ensured me a comfortable retirement. In my circle of friends I'm known as dependable. If someone needs a sitter they know they can call Rebecca. If they need advice or someone to feed their fish while they're on vacation they don't have to worry. I was never late for work, never took five minutes extra for lunch."

"Commendable," he said, and earned a glare.

"Just the type of employee I imagine you'd like to hire."

He swallowed a chuckle. He'd been prepared for her to confess she had a husband, five husbands, a prison record. Instead she was telling him she was an accountant with an excellent work record. "I have no desire to hire you, Rebecca."

"Just as well." She turned away and started to prowl the room again. "You'd undoubtedly change your mind after I tell you the rest."

Stephen crossed his ankles and settled back. God, what a woman she was. "I'm anxious to hear it."

"My aunt died about three months ago, suddenly."

"I'm sorry." He would have gone to her then, but he could see she was far from ready. "I know how difficult it is to lose family."

"She was all I had left." Because she needed something to do, she pushed open the balcony doors. Warm, fragrant night air rushed in. "I couldn't believe she was gone. Just like that. No warning. Of course, I handled the funeral arrangements. No fuss, no frills. Just the way Aunt Jeannie would have wanted. She was a very economical woman, not only in finances but in dress, in speech, in manner. As long as I can remember, people compared me to her."

Stephen's brow lifted again as he studied the woman being buffeted by the breeze—the short red silk robe, the tousled hair.

"Soon after her death—I don't know if it was days or a week—something just snapped. I looked at myself, at my life, and I hated it." She dragged her hair back, only to have the wind catch it again. "I was a good employee, just like my aunt, a good credit risk, a dependable friend. Law-abiding, conservative and boring. Suddenly I could see myself ten, twenty, thirty years down the road, with nothing more than I had at that moment. I couldn't stand it."

She turned around. The breeze caught at the hem of her robe and sent it dancing around her legs. "I quit my job, and I sold everything."

"Sold?"

"Everything I owned—car, apartment, furniture, books, absolutely everything. I turned all the cash into traveler's checks, even the small inheritance from my aunt. Thousands of dollars. I know it might not sound like a lot to you, but it was more than I'd ever imagined having at once."

"Wait." He held up a hand, wanting to be certain he understood everything. "You're telling me that you sold your possessions, *all* your possessions?"

She couldn't remember ever having felt more foolish, and she straightened her shoulders defensively. "Right down to my coffeepot."

"Amazing," he murmured.

"I bought new clothes, new luggage, and flew to London. First-class. I'd never been on a plane before in my life."

"You'd never flown, but took your first trip across the Atlantic."

She didn't hear the admiration in his voice, only the amusement. "I wanted to see something different. To *be* something different. I stayed at the Ritz and took pictures of the changing of the guard. I flew to Paris and had my hair cut." Self-consciously she lifted a hand to it.

Because he could see that she was overwrought, he was careful not to smile. "You flew to Paris for a haircut."

"I'd heard some women discussing this stylist, and I— Never mind." It was no use trying to explain that she'd gone to the same hairdresser, to the same shops, for years. The same everything. "Right after Paris, I came here," she went on. "I met you. Things happened. I let them happen." Tears threatened. She could only pray he didn't see them. "You were exciting, and attracted to me. Or attracted to who you thought I was. I'd never had a romance. No one had ever looked at me the way you did."

Once more he chose his words carefully. "Are you saying that being with me was different? An adventure, like flying to a Paris salon?"

She would never be able to explain what being with him had meant to her. "Apologies and explanations really don't make any difference now. But I am sorry, Stephen. I'm sorry for everything."

He didn't see the tears, but he heard the regret in her voice. His eyes narrowed. His muscles tensed. "Are you apologizing for making love with me, Rebecca?"

"I'm apologizing for whatever you like. I'd make it up to you if I could, but I don't know how, unless I jump out the window."

He paused, as if he were considering it. "I don't think this requires anything quite that drastic. Perhaps if you'd sit down calmly?"

She shook her head and stayed where she was. "I can't handle any more of this tonight, Stephen. I'm sorry. You've every right to be angry."

He rose, the familiar impatience building. But she was so pale, looked so fragile, sounded so weary. He hadn't treated her gently before. At least he could do so now.

"All right. Tomorrow, then, after you've rested." He started to go to her, then checked himself. It would take time to show her that there were other ways to love. Time to convince her that love was more, much more than an adventure. "I want you to know that I regret what happened tonight. But that, too, will wait until tomorrow." Though he wanted to touch a hand to her cheek, he kept it fisted in his pocket. "Get some rest."

She had thought her heart was already broken. Now it shattered. Not trusting her voice, she nodded.

He left her alone. The door scraped against the splintered jamb as he secured it. She supposed there might have been a woman somewhere who'd made a bigger fool of herself. At the moment, it didn't seem to matter.

At least there was something she could do for both of them. Disappear.

CHAPTER 10

It was her own fault, she supposed. There were at least half a dozen promising accounting positions in the want ads. Not one of them interested her. Rebecca circled them moodily. How could she be interested in dental plans and profit sharing? All she could think about, all she'd been able to think about for two weeks, was Stephen.

What had he thought when he'd found her gone? Relief? Perhaps a vague annoyance at business left unfinished? Pen in hand, Rebecca stared out of the window of the garden apartment she'd rented. In her fantasies she imagined him searching furiously for her, determined to find her, whatever the cost. Reality, she thought with a sigh, wasn't quite so romantic. He would have been relieved. Perhaps she wasn't sophisticated, but at least she'd stepped out of his life with no fuss.

Now it was time to get her own life in order.

First things first. She had an apartment, and the little square of lawn outside the glass doors was going to make her happy. That in itself was a challenge. Her old condo had been centrally located on the fifth floor of a fully maintained modern building.

This charming and older development was a good thirty miles from downtown, but she could hear the birds in the morning. She would be able to look out at old oaks and sweeping maples and flowers she would plant herself. Perhaps it wasn't as big a change as a flight to Paris, but for Rebecca it was a statement.

She'd bought some furniture. *Some* was the operative word. Thus far she'd picked out a bed, one antique table and a single chair.

Not logical, Rebecca thought with a faint smile. No proper and economical living room suite, no tidy curtains. Even the single set of towels she'd bought was frivolous. And exactly what she'd wanted. She would do what she'd secretly wanted to do for years—buy a piece here, a piece there. Not because it was a good buy or durable, but because she wanted it.

She wondered how many people would really understand the satisfaction of making decisions not because they were sensible but because they were desirable. She'd done it with her home, her wardrobe. Even with her hair, she thought, running a hand through it. Outward changes had led to inner changes. Or vice versa. Either way, she would never again be the woman she'd been before.

Or perhaps she would be the woman she'd always been but had refused to acknowledge.

Then why was she circling ads in the classifieds? Rebecca asked herself. Why was she sitting here on a beautiful morning planning a future she had no interest in? Perhaps it was true that she would never have the one thing, the one person, she really wanted. There would be no more picnics or walks in the moonlight or frantic nights in bed. Still, she had the memories, she had the moments, she had the dreams. There would be no regrets where Stephen was concerned. Not now, and not ever. And if she was now more the woman she had been with him, it had taken more than a change in hairstyle.

She was stronger. She was surer. She was freer. And she'd done it herself.

She could think of nothing she wanted less than to go back into someone else's firm, tallying figures, calculating profit and loss. So she wouldn't. Rebecca sank into the chair as the thought struck home.

She wouldn't. She wouldn't go job hunting, carrying her résumé, rinsing sweaty palms in the rest room, putting her career and life in someone else's hands again. She'd open her own firm. A small one, certainly. Personalized. Exclusive, she decided, savoring the word.

Why not? She had the skill, the experience, and—finally—she had the courage.

It wouldn't be easy. In fact, it would be risky. The money she had left would have to go toward renting office space, equipment, a phone system, advertising. With a bubbling laugh, she sprang up and searched for a legal pad and a pencil. She had to make lists—not only of things to do but of people to call. She had enough contacts from her McDowell, Jableki and Kline days. Maybe, just maybe, she could persuade some of her former clients to give her a try.

"Just a minute," she called out when she heard the knock on the door. She scribbled a reminder to look for file cabinets as she went to answer. She'd much rather have some good solid oak file cabinets than a living room sofa.

She knew better than to open the door without checking the security peephole, but she was much too involved with her plans to think about such things. When she opened the door, she found herself face-to-face with Stephen.

Even if she could have spoken, he wasn't in the mood to let her. "What in the hell do you think you're doing?" he demanded as he slammed the door behind him. "Do you deliberately try to drive me mad, or does it come naturally to you?"

"I—I don't—" But he was already yanking her against

him. Whatever words she might have spoken dissolved
into a moan against his lips. Her pad fell to the floor with
a slap. Even as her arms came up around him he was
thrusting her away.

"What kind of game are you playing, Rebecca?"
When she just shook her head, he dug his hands into
his pockets and paced the wide, nearly empty room. He
was unshaven, disheveled and absolutely gorgeous. "It's
taken me two weeks and a great deal of trouble to find
you. I believe we'd agreed to talk again. I was surprised
to discover you'd not only left Athens, but Europe." He
swung back and pinned her with a look. "Why?"

Still reeling from his entrance, she struggled not to
babble. "I thought it best that I leave."

"You thought?" He took a step toward her, his fury
so palatable that she braced herself. "You thought it
best," he repeated. "For whom?"

"For you. For both of us." She caught herself fiddling
with the lapels of her robe and dropped her hands. "I
knew you were angry with me for lying to you and that
you regretted what had happened between us. I felt it
would be better for both of us if I—"

"Ran away?"

Her chin came up fractionally. "Went away."

"You said you loved me."

She swallowed. "I know."

"Was that another lie?"

"Please don't." She turned away, but there was no-where to go. "Stephen, I never expected to see you again. I'm trying to make some sense out of my life, to do things in a way that's not only right but makes me happy. In Greece, I guess, I did what made me happy, but I didn't think about what was right. The time with you was…"

"Was what?"

Dragging both hands through her hair, she turned to him again. It was as if the two weeks had never been. She was facing him again, trying to explain what she feared she could never explain. "It was the best thing that ever happened to me, the most important, the most unforgettable, the most precious. I'll always be grateful for those few days."

"Grateful." He wasn't sure whether to laugh or mur-der her. Stepping forward, he surprised them both by slipping his hands lightly around her throat. "For what? For my giving you your first fling? A fast, anonymous romance with no consequences?"

"No." She lifted a hand to his wrist but made no at-tempt to struggle. "Did you come all this way to make me feel more guilty?"

"I came all this way because I finish what I begin. We'd far from finished, Rebecca."

"All right." Be calm, she told herself. When a man was this close to the edge, a woman's best defense was serenity. "If you'll let me go, we'll talk. Would you like some coffee?"

His fingers tightened reflexively, then slowly relaxed. "You've bought a new pot."

"Yes." Was that humor in his eyes? she wondered. "There's only one chair. Why don't you use it while I go into the kitchen?"

He took her arm. "I don't want coffee, or a chair, or a pleasant conversation."

It seemed serenity wouldn't work. "All right, Stephen. What do you want?"

"You. I'd thought I'd made that fairly obvious." When she frowned, he glanced around the apartment. "Now tell me, Rebecca, is this what you want? A handful of rooms to be alone in?"

"I want to make the best of the rest of my life. I've already apologized for deceiving you. I realize that—"

"Deceiving me." He held up a finger to stop her. "I've wanted to clear that point up myself. How did you deceive me?"

"By letting you think that I was something I'm not."

"You're not a beautiful, interesting woman? A passionate woman?" He lifted a brow as he studied her. "Rebecca, I have too much pride to ever believe you could deceive me that completely."

He was confusing her—deliberately, she was sure. "I told you what I'd done."

"What you'd done," he agreed. "And how you'd done it." He brought his hand to her throat again, this time in a caress. His anger hadn't made her knees weak. She felt them tremble now at his tenderness. "Selling your possessions and flying to Paris for a new hairstyle. Quitting your job and grabbing life with both hands. You fascinate me." Her eyes stayed open wide when he brushed his lips over hers. "I think the time is nearly over when you'll be so easily flattered. It's almost a pity." He drew her closer, slowly, while his mouth touched hers. Relief coursed through him as he felt her melt and give. "Do you think it was your background that attracted me?"

"You were angry," she managed.

"Yes, angry at the idea that I had been part of your experiment. Furious," he added before he deepened the kiss. "Furious that I had been of only passing interest." She was heating in his arms, just as he remembered, just as he needed, softening, strengthening. "Shall I tell you how angry? Shall I tell you that for two weeks I couldn't work, couldn't think, couldn't function, because you were everywhere I looked and nowhere to be found?"

"I had to go." She was already tugging at his shirt to find the flesh beneath. To touch him again, just for a moment. To be touched by him. "When you said you regretted making love…" Her own words brought her back. Quickly she dropped her hands and stepped away.

He stared at her for a moment, then abruptly swore and began to pace. "I've never thought myself this big a fool. I hurt you that night in a much different way than I'd believed. Then I handled it with less finesse than I might the most unimportant business transaction." He paused, sighing. For the first time she saw clearly how incredibly weary he was.

"You're tired. Please, sit down. Let me fix you something."

He took a moment to press his fingers to his eyes. Again he wanted to laugh—while he strangled her. She was exactly what he needed, what he understood. Yet at the same time she baffled him.

"You weaken me, Rebecca, and bring out the fool I'd forgotten I could be. I'm surprised you allowed me to set foot into your home. You should have—" As quickly as the anger had come, it faded. As quickly as the tension had formed, it eased. Everything he'd needed to see was in her eyes. Carefully now, he drew a deep breath. A man wasn't always handed so many chances at happiness.

"Rebecca, I never regretted making love with you." He stopped her from turning with the lightest of touches on her shoulder. "I regretted only the way it happened. Too much need and too little care. I regret, I'll always regret, that for your first time there was fire but no warmth." He took her hands in his and brought them to his lips.

"It was beautiful."

"In its way." His fingers tightened on hers. Still so innocent, he thought. Still so generous. "It was not kind or patient or tender, as love should be the first time."

She felt hope rise in her heart again. "None of that mattered."

"It mattered, more than I can ever tell you. After, when you told me everything, it only mattered more. If I had done what my instincts told me to do that night you would never have left me. But I thought you needed time before you could bear to have me touch you again." Slowly, gently, he drew the tip of her finger into his mouth and watched her eyes cloud over. "Let me show you what I should have shown you then." With her hands locked in his, he looked into her eyes. "Do you want me?"

It was time for the truth. "Yes."

He lifted her into his arms and heard her breath catch. "Do you trust me?"

"Yes."

When he smiled, her heart turned over. "Rebecca, I must ask you one more thing."

"What is it?"

"Do you have a bed?"

She felt her cheeks heat even as she laughed. "In there."

She was trembling. It reminded him how careful he had to be, how precious this moment was to both of them.

The sun washed over the bed, over them, as he lay beside her. And kissed her—only kissed her, softly, deeply, thoroughly, until her arms slipped from around him to fall bonelessly to her sides. She trembled still as he murmured to her, as his lips brushed over her cheeks, her throat.

He had shown her the desperation love could cause, the sharp-edged pleasure, the speed and the fury. Now he showed her that love could mean serenity and sweetness.

And she showed him.

He had thought to teach her, not to learn, to reassure her but not to be comforted. But he learned, and he was comforted. The need was there, as strong as it had been the first time. But strength was tempered with patience. As he slipped his hands down her robe to part it, to slide it away from her skin, he felt no need to hurry. He could delight in the way the sun slanted across her body, in the way her flesh warmed to his touch.

Her breath was as unsteady as her hands as she undressed him. But not from nerves. She understood that now. She felt strong and capable and certain. Anticipation made her tremble. Pleasure made her shudder. She gave a sigh that purred out of her lips as she arched against his seeking hands. Then he nipped lightly at her breast and she bounded from serenity to passion in one breathless leap.

Still he moved slowly, guiding her into a kind of heated torment she'd never experienced. Desire boiled in her, and his name sprang to her lips and her body coiled like a spring. Chaining down his own need, he set hers free and watched as she flew over the first peak.

"Only for me," he murmured as she went limp in his arms. "Only for me, Rebecca." With his own passions strapped, he slipped into her, determined to watch her build again. "Tell me you love me. Look at me and tell me."

She opened her eyes. She could barely breathe. Somehow the strength was pouring back into her, but so fast, so powerfully. Sensation rolled over sensation, impossibly. She moved with him, pressed center to center, heart to heart, but all she could see were his eyes, so dark, so blue, so intense. Perhaps she was drowning in them.

"I love you, Stephen."

Then she was falling, fathoms deep, into his eyes, into the sea. With her arms locked around him, she dragged him under with her.

He pulled her against him so that he could stroke her hair and wait for his pulse to level. She'd been innocent. But the surprise, the one he'd been dealing with for weeks, was that until Rebecca he'd been just as innocent. He'd known passion, but he'd never known intimacy, not the kind that reached the heart as fully as the body. And yet...

"We've been here before," he murmured. "Do you feel it, too?"

She linked her fingers with his. "I never believed in things like that until you. When I'm with you it's like remembering." She lifted her head to look at him. "I can't explain it."

"I love you, Rebecca, only more knowing who you are, why you are."

She touched a hand to his cheek. "I don't want you to say anything you don't really feel."

"How can a woman be so intelligent and still so stupid?" With a shake of his head, Stephen rolled on top of her. "A man doesn't travel thousands of miles for this, however delightful it may be. I love you, and though it annoyed me for quite some time I'm accustomed to it now."

"Annoyed you."

"Infuriated." He kissed her to cut off whatever retort she might make. "I'd seen myself remaining free for years to come. Then I met a woman who sold her coffeepot so she could take pictures of goats."

"I certainly have no intention of interfering with your plans."

"You already have." He smiled, holding her still when she tried to struggle away. "Marriage blocks off certain freedoms and opens others."

"Marriage?" She stopped struggling but turned her head to avoid another kiss.

"Soon." He nuzzled her neck. "Immediately."

"I never said I'd marry you."

"No, but you will." With his fingertips only, he began to arouse her. "I'm a very persuasive man."

"I need to think." But she was trembling again. "Stephen, marriage is very serious."

"Deadly. And I should warn you that I've already decided to murder any man you look at for more than twenty seconds."

"Really?" She turned her head back, prepared to be angry. But he was smiling. No one else had ever smiled at her in quite that way. "Really?"

"I can't let you go, Rebecca. Can't and won't. Come back with me. Marry me. Have children with me."

"Stephen—"

He laid a finger to her lips. "I know what I'm asking you. You've already started a new life, made new plans. We've had only days together, but I can make you happy. I can promise to love you for a lifetime, or however many lifetimes we have. You once dived into the sea on impulse. Dive with me now, Rebecca. I swear you won't regret it."

Gently she pressed her lips to his fingertip, then drew his hand away. "All my life I've wondered what I might find if I had the courage to look. I found you, Stephen." With a laugh she threw her arms around him. "When do you want to leave?"

* * * * *

THE BEST MISTAKE

CHAPTER 1

No one answered the door. Coop glanced at the scrawled note in his hand to make sure he had the right address. It checked out, and since the tidy two-story Tudor in the neat, tree-lined neighborhood was precisely what he was after, he knocked again. Loudly.

There was a car in the drive, an aging station wagon that could use a good wash and a little bodywork. Somebody was in there, he thought, scowling up at the second-floor window, where music pumped out— high-volume rock with a thumping backbeat. He stuffed the note and his hands in his pockets and took a moment to survey the surroundings.

The house was trim, set nicely off the road behind clipped bayberry hedges. The flower garden, in which spring blossoms were beginning to thrive, was both colorful and just wild enough not to look static.

Not that he was a big flower lover, but there *was* something to be said for ambience.

There was a shiny red tricycle beside the driveway, and that made him a little uneasy. He wasn't particularly fond of kids. Not that he disliked them. It was just that they always seemed a kind of foreign entity to him, like aliens from an outlying planet: they spoke a different language, had a different culture. And, well, they were short, and usually sticky.

Still, the ad had talked of quiet, privacy, and a convenient distance from Baltimore. That was exactly what he was looking for.

He knocked again, only to have a thundering wave of music wash out the window over him. The rock didn't bother him. At least he understood it. But he wasn't a man to kick his heels outside a closed door for long, so he tried the knob.

When it turned, he pushed the door open and walked in. In an old habit, he pushed back the dark hair that fell over his forehead and scanned the none-too-neat living room he'd entered.

There was a lot of clutter, and he, a bachelor who'd spent a great deal of his thirty-two years living alone, wondered over it. He wasn't fussy or obsessive, he often told himself. It was simply that everything had a place, and it was easier to find if it had been put there. Obviously his prospective landlord didn't agree.

There were toys that went along with the tricycle outside, piles of magazines and newspapers, a pint-size fielder's cap that declared for the O's.

At least the kid had taste, Coop decided, and moved on.

There was a small powder room done in an amazing combination of purple and green, and a den that had been converted into a makeshift office. File drawers were open, papers spilling out. In the kitchen dishes waited in the sink to be washed, and lurid drawings, created by a child with a wild imagination, decorated the front of the refrigerator.

Maybe, he thought, it was just as well no one had answered the door.

He considered backtracking and wandering upstairs. As long as he was here, it made sense to check the rest of the place out. Instead, he stepped outside to get the lay of the land. He spotted open wooden steps leading to a short deck. The private entrance the ad had mentioned, he mused, and climbed.

The glass door was open, and the music rolling through it was overwhelming. He caught the smell of fresh paint, one he'd always enjoyed, and stepped inside.

The open area combined kitchen and living space cleverly enough. The appliances weren't new, but they were gleaming. The tile floor had been scrubbed recently enough for him to identify pine cleaner beneath the scent of paint.

Feeling more hopeful, he followed the music, snooping a bit as he went. The bathroom was as scrupulously clean as the kitchen, and, fortunately, a plain glossy white. Beside the sink was a book on home repair, open to the plumbing section. Wary, Coop turned on the tap. When the water flowed out fast and clear, he nodded, satisfied.

A small room with definite office potential and a nice view of the yard was across the hall. The ad had claimed two bedrooms.

The music led him to it, a fair-sized room that fronted the house, with space enough for his California king. The floor, which seemed to be a random-width oak in good condition, was covered with splattered drop cloths. There were paint cans, trays, brushes, extra rollers. A laborer in baggy overalls and bare feet completed the picture. Despite the hair-concealing cap and oversize denim, Coop recognized a woman when he saw one.

She was tall, and the bare feet on the stepladder were long and narrow and decorated with paint splotches and hot-pink toenails. She sang, badly, along with the music.

Coop rapped on the door jamb. "Excuse me."

She went on painting, her hips moving rhythmically as she started on the ceiling border. Stepping across the drop cloths, Coop tapped her on the back.

She screamed, jumped and turned all at once.

Though he was quick on his feet, he wasn't fast enough to avoid the slap of the paintbrush across his cheek.

He swore and jerked backward, then forward again to catch her before she tumbled off the ladder. He had a quick, and not unpleasant, impression of a slim body, a pale, triangular face dominated by huge, long-lashed brown eyes, and the scent of honeysuckle.

Then he was grunting and stumbling backward, clutching the stomach her elbow had jammed into. She yelled something while he fought to get his breath back.

"Are you crazy?" he managed, then shot up a hand as she hefted a can, slopping paint over the sides as she prepared to use it as a weapon. "Lady, if you throw that at me, I'm going to have to hurt you."

"What?" she shouted.

"I said, don't throw that. I'm here about the ad."

"What?" she shouted again. Her eyes were still wide and full of panic, and she looked capable of anything.

"The ad, damn it." Still rubbing his stomach, Coop marched to the portable stereo and shut it off. "I'm here about the ad," he repeated, his voice loud in the sudden silence.

The big brown eyes narrowed with suspicion. "What ad?"

"The apartment." He swiped a hand over his cheek,

studied the smear of white on it, and swore again. "The apartment."

"Really?" She kept her eyes glued to his. He looked tough, she thought. Like a brawler with those broad shoulders, lean athletic build and long legs. His eyes, a light, almost translucent green, looked anything but friendly, and the faded Baltimore Orioles T-shirt and battered jeans didn't contribute any sense of respectability. She figured she could outrun him, and she could certainly outscream him. "The ad doesn't start to run until tomorrow."

"Tomorrow?" Nonplussed, he reached into his pocket for his scribbled note. "This is the right address. The ad was for this place."

She stood her ground. "It doesn't run until tomorrow, so I don't see how you could know about it."

"I work at the paper." Moving cautiously, he held out the note. "Since I've been looking for a place, I asked one of the girls in Classifieds to keep an eye out." He glanced down at his note again. "Two-bedroom apartment on second floor, private entrance, quiet neighborhood convenient for commuters."

She only continued to frown at him. "That's right."

Realizing his inside track wasn't strictly ethical, he winced. "Look, I guess she got a little overenthusiastic. I gave her a couple of tickets to a game, and she must've figured she'd do me a favor and pass the information along a little early."

When he saw that her grip on the can had relaxed, he tried a smile. "I knocked, then I came around back." Probably best not to mention he'd wandered through the house first.

"The ad didn't run the address."

"I work at the paper," he repeated. He was taking a good look at her now. There was something vaguely familiar about her face. And what a face it was. All slashing cheekbones and liquid eyes, that creamy porcelain skin women's face cream ads always raved about. Her mouth was wide, with an alluringly full lower lip. At the moment, the face continued to frown.

"They had the address for billing," he continued. "Since I had a couple of hours, I thought I'd come by and check it out. Look, I can come back tomorrow, if you'd feel more comfortable. But I'm here now." He shrugged. "I can show you my press pass."

He pulled it out for her, and was pleased when she narrowed her eyes to study it. "I do a column. J. Cooper McKinnon on sports. 'All in the Game'?"

"Oh." It meant nothing to her. The sports page wasn't her choice of reading material. But the smile had appeased her. He didn't look so much like a thug when he smiled. And the smear of paint decorating the lean, tanned face added just enough comedy to soothe her. "I guess it's all right, then. I wasn't expecting to show the apartment for a couple of days yet. It's not ready." She held up the can, set it down again. "I'm still painting."

"I noticed."

She laughed at that. It was a full-throated, smoky sound that went with the natural huskiness of her voice. "Guess you did. I'm Zoe Fleming." She crouched down to dampen a rag with paint remover.

"Thanks." He rubbed the rag over his cheek. "The ad said immediate occupancy."

"Well, I figured I'd be finished in here by tomorrow, when the ad was scheduled to run. Are you from the area?"

"I've got a place downtown. I'm looking for something with a little more space, a little more atmosphere."

"This is a pretty good-sized apartment. It was converted about eight years ago. The guy who owned it had it done for his son, and when he died, the son sold it and moved to California. He wanted to write sit-coms."

Coop walked over to check out the view. He moved fluidly, Zoe thought, like a man who knew how to stay light and ready on his feet. She'd had the impression of wiry strength when her body tumbled into his. And good strong hands. Quick ones, too. She pursed her lips. It might be handy to have a man around.

"Is it just you, Mr. McKinnon?" She thought wistfully how nice it would be if he had a family—another child for Keenan to play with.

"Just me." The place felt right, he decided. It would be good to get out of a box that was just one more box in a building of boxes, to smell grass now and then. Barbecue smoke. "I can move in over the weekend."

She hadn't thought it would be so easy, and she nibbled her lip as she thought it through. She'd never been a landlady before, but she'd been a tenant, and she figured she knew the ropes. "I'll need first and last months' rent."

"Yeah."

"And, ah, references."

"I'll give you the number of the management company that handles my building. You can call Personnel at the paper. Have you got a lease for me to sign?"

She didn't. She'd checked out a book from the library, and she'd meant to type up a scaled-down copy of a lease from it the next morning. "I'll have it tomorrow. Don't you want to look at the rest of the apartment, ask any questions?" She'd been practicing her landlady routine for days.

"I've seen it. It's fine."

"Well." That deflated her a bit. "I guess I can cancel the ad."

There was a sound like a herd of rampaging elephants.

Zoe glanced toward the open door and crouched to intercept the missile that hurtled through.

It was a boy, Coop saw when she scooped the child up. He had glossy golden hair, red sneakers, and jeans that were streaked with some unidentifiable substance that looked like it would easily transfer to other surfaces. He carried a plastic lunch box with a picture of some apocalyptic space battle on it, and a sheet of drawing paper that was grimy at the edges.

"I drew the ocean," he announced. "And a million people got ate by sharks."

"Gruesome." Zoe shuddered obligingly before accepting his sloppy kiss. She set him down to admire the drawing. "These are really big sharks," she said, cagily distinguishing the shark blobs from the people blobs.

"They're monster sharks. Mutant monster sharks. They have teeth."

"So I see. Keenan, this is Mr. McKinnon. Our new tenant."

Keenan wrapped one arm around Zoe's leg for security as he eyed the stranger. His eyes were working their way up to Coop's face when they lit on the T-shirt. "That's baseball. I'm gonna learn. Mama's getting a book so's she can teach me."

A book. Coop barely checked a snort. As if you could learn the greatest game invented by Man from a book. What kind of nerd did the kid have for a father?

"Great." It was all Coop intended to say. He'd always thought it wise to avoid entangling himself in a conversation with anyone under sixteen.

Keenan had other ideas. "If you're going to live here, you have to pay rent. Then we can pay the mortgage and stuff and go to Disney World."

What *was* the kid? An accountant?

"Okay, old man." Zoe laughed and ruffled his hair. "I can handle it from here. Go on down and put your stuff away."

"Is Beth coming to play with me tonight?"

"Yes, Beth's coming. Now scoot. I'll be down in a minute."

"'Kay." He made a dash for the door, stopping when his mother called him. It only took one look, the raised brow for him to remember. He looked back at Coop, flashed a quick, sunny grin. "Bye, mister."

The herd of elephants rampaged again, then there was the crash of a door slamming. "He makes an entrance," Zoe said as she turned back to Coop. "The dramatic flair comes from my mother. She's an actress, off-off-Broadway." Tilting her head, Zoe rested one bare foot on the bottom rung of the stepladder. "You look like you're ready to change your mind. You have a problem with children?"

"No." The kid might have thrown him off, but Coop doubted it would be a problem. The boy would hardly be beating a path to his door. And if he did, Coop thought, he could send him off again quickly enough. "No, he's, ah, cute."

"Yes, he is. I won't claim he's an angel, but he won't make a nuisance of himself. If he gives you any trouble, just let me know."

"Sure. Look, I'll come by tomorrow to sign the lease and give you a check. I'll pick up the keys then."

"That'll be fine."

"Any special time good for you?"

She looked blank for a moment. "What's tomorrow?"

"Friday."

"Friday." She closed her eyes and flipped through her messy internal calendar. "I'm working between ten and two. I think." She opened her eyes again, smiled. "Yeah, I'm pretty sure. Anytime after two-thirty?"

"Fine. Nice meeting you, Mrs. Fleming."

She took his offered hand. "It's Miss," she said easily. "I'm not married. And since we'll be living together, so to speak, you can make it Zoe."

CHAPTER 2

No one answered the door. Again. Coop checked his watch and saw that it was quarter to three. He didn't like to think he was a man obsessed with time, but as his living centered around deadlines, he did respect it. There was no rusting station wagon in the driveway this time, but he walked around the back of the house, hoping. Before he could start up the stairs to the apartment, he was hailed from across the chain-link fence.

"Young man! Yoo-hoo, young man!" Across the yard next door came a flowered muumuu, topped with a curling thatch of brightly hennaed hair that crowned a wide face. The woman hurried to the fence in a whirl of color. It wasn't just the dress and the improbable hair, Coop noted. The face itself was a rainbow of rich red lipstick, pink cheeks and lavender eye shadow.

When she reached the fence, she pressed a many-ringed hand over the wide shelf of her breasts. "Not as young as I used to be," she said. "I'm Mrs. Finkleman."

"Hi."

"You're the young man who's going to live upstairs." Mrs. Finkleman, a born flirt, patted her curls. "Zoe didn't tell me you were so handsome. Single, are you?"

"Yeah," Coop said cautiously. "Miss Fleming was supposed to meet me. She doesn't seem to be home."

"Well, that's Zoe, flying here, flying there." Mrs. Finkleman beamed and leaned comfortably on the fence, as if she were settling in for a nice cozy gossip. "Got a dozen things on her plate at once, that girl does. Having to raise that sweet little boy all alone. Why, I don't know what I'd have done without my Harry when our young ones were coming up."

Coop was a reporter, after all. That, added to the fact that he was curious about his landlady, put him in interview mode. "The kid's father doesn't help out any?"

Mrs. Finkleman snorted. "Don't see hide nor hair of him. From what I'm told, he lit out the minute he found out Zoe was expecting. Left her high and dry, and her hardly more than a child herself. Far as I know, he's never so much as seen the boy. The little sweetheart."

Coop assumed she was referring to Keenan. "Nice kid. What's he, five, six?"

"Just four. Bright as a button. They grow them

smarter these days. Teach them faster, too. The little love's in preschool now. He'll be home any minute."

"His mother went to pick him up, then?"

"Oh, no, not her week for car pool. Alice Miller— that's the white house with blue trim, down the block?— it's her week. She has a boy and a girl. Little darlings. The youngest, Steffie, is Keenan's age. Now her oldest, Brad, there's a pistol for you."

As she began to fill Coop in on the neighborhood rascal, he decided it was time to draw the interview to a close. "Maybe you could tell Miss Fleming I was by? I can leave a number where she can reach me when—"

"Oh, goodness." Mrs. Finkleman waved a hand. "I do run on. Nearly forgot why I came out here in the first place. Zoe called and asked me to look out for you. Got held up at the flower shop. She works there three days a week. That's Floral Bouquet, down in Ellicott City? Nice place, but expensive. Why, it's a crime to charge so much for a daisy."

"She got held up," Coop prompted.

"Her relief had car trouble, so Zoe's going to be a little late. Said you could go right on into the kitchen there, where she left the lease and the keys."

"That's fine. Thanks."

"No problem at all. This is a friendly neighborhood. Always somebody to lend a helping hand. I don't think Zoe mentioned what you did for a living."

"I'm a sportswriter for the *Dispatch*."

"You don't say? Why, my Harry's just wild for sports. Can't budge him from in front of the TV when a game's on."

"That's what makes this country great."

Mrs. Finkleman laughed and gave Coop's arm an affectionate bat that might have felled a lesser man. "You men are all the same. You can come over and talk sports with Harry anytime. Me, if it's not baseball, it isn't worth talking about."

Coop, who'd been about to retreat, brightened. "You like baseball?"

"Son, I'm a Baltimore native." As if that said it all. "Our boys are going to go all the way this year. Mark my word."

"They could do it, if they heat those bats up. The pitching rotation's gold this year, and the infield's tight as a drum. What they need—"

Coop was interrupted by a cheerful toot. He glanced over to see Keenan burst out of a red sedan and rocket across the side yard.

"Hi, mister. Hi, Mrs. Finkleman. Carly Myers fell down, and there was blood." The big brown eyes gleamed wickedly. "Lots and lots of it, and she screamed and cried." He demonstrated, letting go with a piercing yell that had Coop's ears ringing. "Then she got a Band-Aid with stars on it." Keenan thought it would have been worth losing some blood for such a neat badge of honor. "Where's Mama?"

"Little lamb." Mrs. Finkleman leaned over the fence to pinch Keenan's cheek. "She's working a little late. She said you could come stay with me until she gets home."

"Okay." Keenan liked his visits next door, since they always included cookies and a rock on Mrs. Finkleman's wonderfully soft lap. "I gotta put my lunch box away."

"Such a good boy," Mrs. Finkleman cooed. "You come on over when you're done. Why don't you show the nice man inside so he can wait for your mother?"

"Okay."

Before Coop could take evasive action, his hand was clutched by Keenan's. He'd been right, he thought with a wince. It was sticky.

"We've got cookies," Keenan told him, cannily deducing that he could have double his afternoon's treat if he played his cards right.

"Great."

"We baked them ourselves, on our night off." Keenan sent Coop a hopeful look. "They're really good."

"I bet." Coop caught the back door before it could slam shut.

"There." Keenan pointed to a ceramic cookie jar in the shape of a big yellow bird on the counter. "In Big Bird."

"Okay, okay." Since it seemed like the best way to appease the kid, Coop reached in and pulled out a handful of cookies. When he dumped them on the table, Keenan's eyes went as wide as saucers. He could hardly believe his luck.

"You can have one, too." He stuffed an entire chocolate chip deluxe in his mouth and grinned.

"That good, huh?" With a shrug, Coop sampled one himself. The kid, Coop decided after the first bite, knew his cookies. "You'd better get next door."

Keenan devoured another cookie, stalling. "I gotta wash out my thermos, 'cause if you don't, it smells."

"Right." Cooper sat at the table to read through the lease while the boy dragged a stool in front of the sink.

Keenan squirted dishwashing liquid in the thermos, and then, when he noticed Coop wasn't paying any attention, he squirted some more. And more. He turned the water up high and giggled when soap began to bubble and spew. With his tongue caught between his teeth, he jiggled the stopper into the sink and began to play dishwasher.

Coop forgot about him, reading quickly. The lease seemed standard enough, he decided. Zoe had already signed both copies. He dashed his signature across from hers, folded his copy, then set the check he'd already written on the table. He'd picked up the keys and rose to tuck his copy in his pocket when he spotted Keenan.

"Oh, God."

The boy was drenched, head to foot. Soap bubbles

dotted his face and hair. A good-sized puddle was forming on the tile at the base of the stool.

"What are you doing?"

Keenan looked over his shoulder, smiled innocently. "Nothing."

"Look, you've got water everywhere." Coop looked around for a towel.

"Everywhere," Keenan agreed, and, testing the opposition, he slapped his hands in the sink. Water and suds geysered.

"Cut it out! Jeez! Aren't you supposed to be somewhere else?" He grabbed a dish towel and advanced, only to be slapped in the face by the next geyser. His eyes narrowed. "Look, kid—"

He heard the front door slam. Like mother, like son, he thought.

"Keenan?" Zoe called out. "I hope you haven't been into those cookies."

Coop looked at the crumbs on the table, on the floor, floating in the soapy water.

"Oh, hell," he muttered.

"Oh, hell," Keenan echoed, beaming at him. He giggled and danced on his stool. "Hi, Mom."

Zoe, her arms full of day-old irises, took in the scene with one glance. Her son was as wet as a drowned dog, her kitchen looked as though a small hurricane had blown through. Hurricane Keenan, she thought. And her new tenant looked damp, frazzled, and charmingly sheepish.

Like a boy caught with his hand in the cookie jar, she noted, glancing at the telltale crumbs.

"Been playing dishwasher again?" With a calm that baffled Coop, she set the flowers down. "I'm just not sure it's the right career choice, Keen-man."

Keenan fluttered his long, wet lashes. "He wanted cookies."

Coop started to defend himself, then simply scowled at the boy.

"I'm sure he did. Go on into the laundry room and get out of those wet clothes."

"Okay." He jumped from the stool, splashing more water before he zoomed away. He stopped only long enough to give his mother a wet kiss before he disappeared into an adjoining room.

"Sorry I'm late," Zoe said easily, yanking the stopper out of the sink then walking to a cupboard to get a vase.

Coop opened his mouth. He started to explain what had gone on in the past ten minutes, but realized he wasn't at all sure. "I signed the lease."

"I see that. Would you mind putting some water in this?" She held out the vase. "I need to get a mop."

"Sure."

She was probably going to wallop the kid with it, Coop thought, and felt a quick tug of regret and guilt.

But the sounds from the laundry room where she'd dis-appeared weren't those he associated with corporal punishment. They were a young boy's giggles, a wom-an's lusty laugh. Coop stood, a vase of water in his hands, and wondered at it.

"You're standing in a puddle," Zoe commented when she came back with a mop and pail.

"Oh, right." Coop glanced down at his wet hightops, shifted. "Here's your vase."

"Thanks." She tended to her flowers first. "You met Mrs. Finkleman, I hear."

"News travels fast."

"Around here it does." When she handed him a dish-cloth to dry his face with, he caught her scent—much more potent, much more colorful, than the flowers. She was wearing jeans and a baggy T-shirt with Floral Bouquet across the chest. Her hair, he noted, was some elusive shade between brown and blond. She wore it tied back in a jaunty ponytail.

When she lifted her brows, he realized he'd been star-ing. "Sorry. I mean—I'm sorry about the mess."

"Were you playing dishwasher, too?"

"Not exactly." It was impossible not to smile back, to ignore the quick pull of attraction.

It wouldn't be so bad, he mused, having a pretty landlady, sharing the house with her, maybe an occa-sional meal. Or an occasional—

"Mama!" Keenan stood in the doorway, wearing nothing but skin. "I can't find my pants."

"In the basket by the washing machine," she told him, without taking her eyes from Coop's.

He'd forgotten about the kid, let himself fantasize a little before remembering she didn't come as a single. He took a long mental step backward and jingled the keys to his new apartment.

"I've got some boxes out in the car," he told her. "I'm going to move some things in this afternoon."

"That's fine." It was silly to feel disappointed, Zoe thought. Foolish to have felt that fast feminine flutter when she recognized interest in his eyes. More foolish to feel let down because the interest had blanked out when her child called her. "Do you need any help?"

"No, I can handle it. I've got a game to cover tonight, so I'm going to move the rest in tomorrow." He backed toward the door. "Thanks."

"Welcome aboard, Mr. McKinnon."

"Coop," he said as he stepped outside. "It's Coop."

Coop, she thought, leaning on the mop handle. It had seemed like such a good idea to make use of the apartment upstairs. The extra income would take some of the pressure off, and maybe add a few bonuses. Like that trip to Disney World that Keenan wanted so badly.

It had been a risk to buy the house, but she'd wanted her son to grow up in a nice neighborhood, with a yard, maybe a dog when he was a little older. The rental income would take away some of the risk.

But she hadn't realized it could add another, more personal risk. She hadn't realized how awkward it might be to have a tenant who was male, single, and absolutely gorgeous.

She laughed at herself. Dream on, Zoe, she thought. J. Cooper McKinnon was just like the rest, who ran like a hound when they heard the patter of little feet.

Something crashed in the laundry room. She just shook her head.

"Come on, sailor," she called to Keenan. "It's time to swab the deck."

CHAPTER 3

"Pretty good digs, Coop. Really, pretty good." Ben Robbins, a staff reporter for the *Dispatch,* sipped a cold one while surveying Coop's apartment. "I didn't think much of it when we hauled all your junk up here, but it ain't half-bad."

It was a lot better than not half-bad, and Coop knew it. He had everything exactly where he wanted it. The living room was dominated by his long, low-slung sofa of burgundy leather and his big-screen television, so perfect for viewing games. A couple of brass lamps, a nicely worn coffee table scuffed from the heels of the dozens of shoes that had rested on it and a single generous chair completed the formal section of the room.

There was an indoor basketball hoop, small-scaled, for practice—and because shooting a little round ball helped him think. A used pinball machine called Home

Run, a stand that held two baseball bats, his tennis racket and a hockey stick, a pair of old boxing gloves hanging on the wall and a scarred Fooz Ball table made up the recreation area.

Coop wouldn't have called them toys. They were tools.

He'd chosen blinds, rather than curtains, for the windows. Blinds, he thought, that would close out the light if a man decided to treat himself to an afternoon nap.

The bedroom held little other than his bed, a nightstand and another TV. The room was for sleeping—or, if he got lucky, another type of sport.

But it was his office that pleased him most. He could already imagine himself spending hours there at his computer, a game playing on his desktop TV. He'd outfitted it with a big swivel chair, a desk that had just the right number of scars and burns, a fax, a dual-line phone and a VCR—to play back those controversial calls or heart-stopping plays.

With all the plaques and photos and sports memorabilia scattered about, it was home.

His home.

"Looks like the neighborhood bar," Ben said, and stretched out his short, hairy legs. "Where the jocks hang out."

Coop considered that the highest of compliments. "It suits me."

"To the ground," Ben agreed, and toasted Coop with his bottle of beer. "A place where a man can relax, be himself. You know, since I started living with Sheila, I've got little china things all over, and underwear hanging in the bathroom. The other day she comes home with a new bedspread. It's got *flowers* all over. Pink flowers." He winced as he drank. "It's like sleeping in a meadow."

"Hey." With all the smug righteousness of the un-encumbered, Coop propped his feet on the coffee table. "Your choice, pal."

"Yeah, yeah. Too bad I'm nuts about her. And her an Oakland fan, too."

"Takes all kinds. Talk is the A's are trading Remirez."

Ben snorted. "Yeah, yeah, pull the other one, champ."

"That's the buzz." Coop shrugged, took a pull on his own beer. "Sending him to K.C. for Dunbar, and that rookie fielder, Jackson."

"They got to be crazy. Remirez hit .280 last season."

".285," Coop told him. "With twenty-four baggers. Led the team in errors, too."

"Yeah, but with a bat like that… And Dunbar, what's he? Maybe he hit .220?"

"It was .218, but he's like a vacuum cleaner at second. Nothing gets by him. And the kid's got potential. Big, strapping farm boy with an arm like a bullet. They need new blood. Most of the starting lineup's over thirty."

They argued baseball and finished their beers in complete male harmony.

"I've got a game to cover."

"Tonight? I thought the O's were in Chicago until tomorrow."

"They are." Coop pocketed his tape recorder, his pad, a pencil. "I'm covering the college game. There's a hot third baseman who's got the scouts drooling. Thought I'd take a look, cop an interview."

"What a job." Ben hauled himself to his feet. "Going to games, hanging around locker rooms."

"Yeah, it's a rough life." He slung an arm over Ben's shoulders as they headed out. "So, how's the story on neutering pets going?"

"Stuff it, Coop."

"Hey, some of us hang around the pound, some of us hang around the ballpark."

And a hell of a day it was for it, too, Coop thought. Balmy and clear-skied. He could almost smell roasting peanuts and hot dogs.

"While you're hanging around a bunch of sweaty college boys in jockstraps, I'll be snuggled up with a woman."

"Under a flowered bedspread."

"Yeah, but she says flowers make her feel sexy. And I'm here to tell you— My, oh, my..."

When Ben's small, square face went lax, Coop turned. He felt his own jaw drop. And, if he wasn't mistaken, his tongue landed on his shoes.

She was wearing what had to be the shortest skirt ever devised by man. Beneath it were a pair of endless legs that were molded into black fishnet hose. She swayed when she walked. How could she help it, when she stood in black skyscraper heels?

A tiny white bustier exposed a delicious amount of cleavage. Around her neck was a shiny black bow tie that, for reasons utterly inexplicable to Coop, made every male cell in his body sizzle.

Her hair was down, falling straight as a pin to her shoulders in a melding of tones that made him think of wild deer leaping through a sunlit forest.

She stopped, smiled, said something, but his mind had checked out the moment his eyes landed on her legs.

"…if you've settled in okay."

"Ah…" He blinked like a man coming out of a coma. "What?"

"I said I haven't had a chance to check and see if you've settled in okay."

"Fine." He folded his tongue back in his mouth and got a grip on himself. "Just fine."

"Good. Keenan came down with a cold, so things have been hectic. I caught a glimpse of you hauling things up the steps a couple of days ago."

"Hauling," he repeated. "Yeah. Ben," he said when his friend jabbed him. "This is Ben. He's been giving me a hand moving."

"Hi, Ben. I'm Zoe."

"Hi, Zoe," Ben said stupidly. "I'm Ben."

She just smiled. It was the outfit, she knew. As much as she hated it, she couldn't help but be amused by how it affected certain members of the species. "Do you work at the paper, too?"

"Yeah, I'm, ah, doing a story on neutering pets."

"Really?" She almost felt sorry for him, the way his Adam's apple was bobbing. "I'll be sure to look for it. I'm glad you're settling in okay. I've got to get to work."

"You're going out?" Coop said. "In that?"

Her lips twitched. "Well, this is my usual outfit when I'm carpooling, but I thought I'd wear it to work tonight. At Shadows? I'm a waitress. Nice meeting you, Ben."

She walked to her car. No, Coop thought, swayed to it, in those long, lazy strides. They were both still staring when she pulled out of the drive and cruised down the street.

"Your landlady," Ben said in a reverential whisper. "That was your landlady."

"I think it was." She hadn't looked like that when he signed the lease. Beautiful, yes—she'd been beautiful, but in a wholesome, unthreatening sort of way. She hadn't looked so...so... Words failed him. She was a mother, for God's sake, he reminded himself. She wasn't supposed to look like that. "She's got a kid."

"Yeah? What kind?"

"Human, I think."

"Come on."

"A boy," Coop said absently. "This high." He held a hand, palm down, about three feet from the ground.

"She may have a kid, but she's also got legs. This high." Ben waved a hand in front of his own throat. "You got a charmed life, Coop. My landlord's got arms like cinder blocks, and a tattoo of a lizard. You got one who looks like a centerfold."

"She's a mother," Coop said under his breath.

"Well, I wouldn't mind coming home to her for milk and cookies. See you at the sweatshop."

"Sure." Coop stood where he was, frowning at the quiet street. Mothers weren't supposed to look like that, he thought again. They were supposed to look…motherly. Safe. Comfortable. He blew out a breath, willed away the knot in his stomach.

She wasn't *his* mother, he reminded himself.

By midnight, Zoe's feet were screaming. Her back ached, and her arms felt as though she'd been hauling boulders rather than drink trays. She'd deflected six propositions, two of them good-hearted enough to amuse, one of them insulting enough to earn the gentleman in question a bruised instep, courtesy of one of her stiletto heels. The others had been the usual, and easily ignored.

It went with the territory, and it didn't bother her overmuch.

The lounge earned its name from the shadowy effect of neon and all the dim corners. The decor was fifties tacky, and the waitresses were dolled up like old-fashioned mindless floozies to match.

But the tips were excellent, and the clientele, for the most part, harmless.

"Two house wines, white, a Black Russian and a coffee, light." After calling out her order to the bartender, Zoe took a moment to roll her shoulders.

She hoped Beth had gotten Keenan to bed without any fuss. He'd been cranky all day—which meant he was nearly over his sniffles. He'd put up quite a fuss that morning, Zoe remembered, when she'd nixed the idea of him going to school.

Didn't get that from me, she thought. She'd never fussed about not going to school. Now, at twenty-five, she deeply regretted letting her education slide. If she'd applied herself, tried for college, she could have developed a skill, had a career.

Instead, she had a high school diploma she'd barely earned, and was qualified for little more than serving drinks to men whose eyes tried to crawl down her cleavage.

But she wasn't one for regrets. She'd done what she'd done, and she had the greatest prize of all.

Keenan. In a couple of years, she figured, she'd have saved enough that she could turn in her bustier and take a night course. Once she had a few business courses under her belt, she could open her own flower shop. And she wouldn't have to leave Keenan with sitters at night.

She served her drinks, took an order from another table and thanked God her break was coming up in five minutes.

When she saw Coop walk in, her first thought was Keenan. But the sick alarm passed almost as quickly as it had come. Coop was relaxed, obviously scoping the place out. When his eyes met hers, he nodded easily and made his way through the scattered tables.

"I thought I'd stop in for a drink."

"This is the place for it. Do you want to sit at the bar, or do you want a table?"

"A table. Got a minute?"

"At quarter after I've got fifteen of them. Why?"

"I'd like to talk to you."

"Okay. What can I get you?"

"Coffee, black."

"Coffee, black. Have a seat."

He watched her head toward the bar and tried not to dwell on how attractive she looked walking away. He hadn't come in because he wanted a drink, but because she seemed like a nice woman in a tight skirt—spot, he corrected. A tight spot.

Get hold of yourself, Coop, he warned himself. He knew better than to let a pair of long legs cloud his judgment. He'd only come in to ask a few questions, get the full story. That was what he did, and he was good at it. Just as he was good at dissecting a game, any game, and finding those small triumphs and small mistakes that influenced the outcome.

"We've been busy tonight." Zoe set two coffees on the table before sliding onto a chair across from Coop. She let out a long, heartfelt sigh, then smiled. "This is the first time I've been off my feet in four hours."

"I thought you worked in a flower shop."

"I do, three days a week." She slid her cramped feet out of her shoes. "Around Mother's Day, Christmas, Easter—you know, the big flower days, I can squeeze in more." She sipped the coffee she'd loaded with sugar and let it pump into her system. "It's just a small shop, and Fred—that's the owner—only keeps on a couple of part-timers. That way he doesn't have to pay any of the bennies, like hospitalization, sick leave."

"That's lousy."

"Hey, it's a job. I like it. It's just Fred and Martha—she's his wife. They've taught me a lot about flowers and plants."

Someone pumped quarters into the juke. The room heated up with music. Coop leaned over the table so that she could hear him. For a moment he lost the thread somewhere in her big brown eyes.

"Have I met you somewhere before?" he asked her.

"In the apartment."

"No, I mean…" He shook his head, let it go. "Uh, why here?"

"Why here what?"

"Why do you work here?"

She blinked, those long lashes fluttering down, thcn up. "For a paycheck."

"It doesn't seem like you should be working in a bar."

"Excuse me?" Zoe wasn't sure if she should be amused or insulted. She chose the former simply because it was her nature. "Do you have a problem with cocktail waitresses?"

"No, no. It's just that, you're a mother."

"Yes, I am. I have a son to prove it." She laughed and leaned her chin on her fist. "Are you thinking it would be more appropriate for me to be home baking cookies or knitting a scarf?"

"No." Though it embarrassed him that he did. "It's that outfit," he blurted out. "And the way all these men look at you."

"If a woman's going to wear something like this, men

are going to look. Looking's all they do," she added. "If it makes you feel better, I don't dress like this for PTA meetings."

He was feeling more ridiculous every second. "Look, it's none of my business. I just have a habit of asking questions. Seems to me you could do better than this. I mean, you've got the flower job, and the rent—"

"And I have a mortgage, a son who seems to outgrow his clothes and shoes every other week, a car payment, grocery bills, doctor bills."

"Doctor? Is the kid sick?"

Zoe rolled her eyes. Just when she was starting to get irritated, he deflated her. "No. Kids Keenan's age are always bringing some germ or other home from school. He needs regular checkups with his pediatrician, with the dentist. Those things aren't free."

"No, but there are programs. Assistance." He stopped, because those big brown eyes had turned fierce.

"I'm perfectly capable of earning a living, and of taking care of my child."

"I didn't mean—"

"Maybe I don't have a college degree or any fancy skills, but I can pay my own way, and my son doesn't lack for anything." She jammed her feet into the back-breaking heels and stood. "We've been doing just fine on our own, and I don't need some nosy jock reporter coming in here and telling me how to be a mother. Coffee's on the house, you jerk."

He winced as she stormed away from the table, then let out a long breath. Handled that one *real* well, Coop.

He wondered if there would be an eviction notice on his door in the morning.

CHAPTER 4

She didn't kick him out. She had thought of it, but had decided the satisfaction she'd gain didn't quite equal the rental income. Besides, she'd heard it all before.

One of the reasons she'd moved from New York was that she'd grown impossibly weary of friends and family telling her how to run her life. How to raise her son.

Baltimore had been a clean slate.

She'd had enough money put aside to afford a nice two-bedroom apartment and invest the rest. And because she was willing to work at any job, and work hard, she'd rarely been unemployed. It had been difficult for her to put Keenan in day-care. But he'd thrived. He had his mother's knack for making friends.

Now, two years after the move, she had a house, and a yard, in the kind of neighborhood she wanted for her son. And she'd paid for every bit of it on her own.

Too many people had told her she was crazy, that she was too young, that she was throwing her life and her chances away. With a grunt, Zoe shoved the lawn mower around and began to cut another strip of grass. *Her* grass, she thought with clenched teeth.

She'd proved them wrong. She'd had her baby, kept her baby, and she was making a decent life for him. She and Keenan weren't statistics. They were a family.

They didn't need anyone to feel sorry for them, or to offer handouts. She was taking care of everything, one step at a time. And she had plans. Good, solid plans.

The tap on her shoulder made her jump. When she whipped her head around and looked at Coop, her hands tightened on the mower. "What?"

"I want to apologize," he shouted. When she only continued to glare at him, he reached down and shut off the engine. "I want to apologize," he repeated. "I was out of line last night."

"Really?"

"I'm sort of addicted to poking into other people's business."

"Maybe you should go cold turkey." She reached down to grab the pull cord. His hand closed over hers. She stared at it a moment. He had big hands, rough-palmed. She remembered the impression she'd gotten of strength and energy. Now the hand was gentle and hard to resist.

She hadn't felt a man's hands—hadn't wanted to feel a man's hands—in a very long time.

"Sometimes I push the wrong buttons," Coop continued. He was staring at their hands, as well, thinking how small hers felt under his. How soft. "It's earned me a fist in the face a time or two." He tried a smile when her gaze slid up to his.

"That doesn't surprise me."

She didn't smile back, but he sensed a softening. The roar of the mower had awakened him. When he'd looked out and seen her marching along behind it in baggy shorts, a T-shirt and a ridiculous straw hat, he'd wanted to go back to bed. But he'd been compelled to seek her out.

It was only a flag of truce, he told himself. After all, he had to live with her. More or less.

"I didn't mean to be critical. I was curious about you. And the kid," he added quickly. "And maybe seeing you in that outfit last night pushed a few of my buttons."

She lifted a brow. That was honest enough, she thought. "All right. No permanent damage."

It had been easier than he'd expected. Coop decided to press his luck. "Listen, I've got to cover the game this afternoon. Maybe you'd like to come along. It's a nice day for baseball."

She supposed it was. It was warm and sunny, with a nice, freshening breeze. There were worse ways to spend the day than in a ballpark with an attractive man who was doing his best to pry his foot out of his mouth.

"It sounds like fun—if I didn't have to work. But Keenan would love it." She watched his jaw drop, and smothered a smile.

"Keenan? You want me to take him?"

"I can't think of anything he'd rather do. Some of the kids play in their yards, and they let him chase the ball. But he's never seen the real thing, except on TV." She smiled now, guilelessly, and held back a hoot of laughter. She could all but see Coop's mind working.

"I don't know too much about kids," he said, back-pedaling cautiously.

"But you know about sports. It'll be great for Keenan to experience his first real game with an expert. When are you leaving?"

"Ah…a couple of hours."

"I'll make sure he's ready. This is awfully nice of you." While he stood staring, she leaned over and kissed his cheek. After one hard tug, she had the mower roaring again.

Coop stood planted like a tree when she strolled away. What the hell was he supposed to do with a kid all afternoon?

He bought popcorn, hot dogs and enormous cups of soft drinks. Coop figured food would keep the kid quiet. Keenan had bounced on the seat of the car throughout the drive to Camden Yards, and since they had arrived he'd goggled at everything.

Coop had heard "What's that?" and "How come?" too many times to count. Nervous as a cat, he settled into the press box with his laptop.

"You can watch through the window here," he instructed Keenan. "And you can't bother anybody, because they're working."

"Okay." Almost bursting with excitement, Keenan clutched his hot dog.

There were lots of people in the press box, some with neat computers, like Coop, others with headphones. A few of them had smiled at him, and all of them had said hello to Coop. Keenan knew Coop was important. As his mother had instructed, he kept close and didn't ask for any presents. Even though there had been really neat stuff at the stands. His mother had given him five whole dollars and told him he could buy a souvenir. But there'd been so many he didn't know which to pick. And Coop had walked so fast he'd hardly been able to look.

But it didn't matter, because he was at a real ball game.

Wide-eyed, he stared down at the field. It was bigger than anything he'd imagined. He knew where the pitcher would stand, and he recognized home plate, but he wasn't sure of anything else.

The big scoreboard exploded with pictures, and words he couldn't read. Circling it all were the stands, filled with more people than he'd ever seen.

When they announced the lineup, he looked down at the players with naked admiration. The national anthem began, and, recognizing it, Keenan stood up, as he'd been taught.

Coop glanced over, saw the boy standing, with a hot dog in one hand and a big, dazzling grin on his face. Suddenly he remembered his first time at a ballpark. His eager hand gripping his father's, his eyes trying to see everything at once, and his heart so full of the excitement, of the game, of just being a boy.

As the players took the field, Coop reached over and tugged on Keenan's bright hair. "Pretty cool, huh?"

"It's the best ever. Those are our guys, right?"

"Those are our guys. They're gonna kick butt."

Keenan giggled and leaned closer to the glass to watch the first pitch. "Kick butt," he said with relish.

He didn't, as Coop had expected, fidget, whine or make a general nuisance of himself. Because he was accustomed to working under noisy and confusing conditions, Keenan's constant questions didn't annoy him overmuch. At least, he thought, the kid had the good sense to ask.

Between innings, Keenan peered over Coop's shoulder and sounded out the words that were popping up on the computer screen, and he did transfer some mustard from his hands onto Coop's sleeve. But it wasn't the disaster Coop had envisioned.

Coop even felt a quick tug of pride when the play-by-play announcer called Keenan over and let the boy sit in his lap for an inning.

Most kids would've been running around the booth begging for more candy. But this one, Coop thought, had come for the game.

"How come he didn't run all the way? How come he didn't?" Keenan shifted from foot to foot. His bladder was past full, but he couldn't bear to miss a minute.

"The throw went to second, so he was forced out," Coop explained. "See, the second baseman caught the ball and stepped on the bag to retire the side."

"Retire the side," Keenan repeated reverently. "But we're still winning?"

"The O's are up by one going into the top of the ninth. Looking at the batting order, I'd say they'll put in a southpaw."

"Southpaw," Keenan repeated, as if it were gospel.

"A left-handed reliever. Probably Scully." He glanced over and noted that Keenan was holding his crotch. "Uh, got a problem?"

"Nuh-uh."

"Let's hit the john—the bathroom." He took Keenan's hand and hoped it wasn't too late. As they passed through the door, Scully was announced as the relief.

"Just like you said." Keenan looked up at Coop with dazzling admiration. "You're smarter than anybody."

Coop felt a grin break out over his face. "Let's just say I know the game."

When they arrived home, Keenan was wearing a new Orioles jersey and carrying an autographed baseball in a pint-size baseball glove. He waved a pennant in his other hand as he scrambled up the steps.

"Look! Look what Coop got me!" He barreled into his mother who'd barely walked in the door herself. "We went into the locker room with the real Orioles, and they signed the baseball for me. To keep."

"Let's see." She took the ball and examined it. "This is really special, Keenan."

"I'm gonna keep it forever. And I got this shirt, too, like they wear. And a glove. It even fits."

Emotion backed up in her throat. "It certainly does. Looks like you're all ready to play ball."

"I'm gonna play third base, 'cause it's the…the…"

"Hot corner," Coop supplied.

"Yeah. Can I go show Mr. Finkleman? Can I show him my baseball?"

"Sure."

"He's gonna be surprised." He turned and threw his

arms around Coop's legs. "Thanks, thanks for taking me. I liked it best of anything. Can we go again, and take Mama?"

"Uh, yeah, I guess. Sure." Feeling awkward again, he patted Keenan's head.

"Okay!" Giving Coop one last squeeze, Keenan raced out the door to show off his treasures.

"You didn't have to buy him all that stuff," Zoe began. "Taking him was enough."

"No big deal. He didn't ask for it, or anything." Coop stuck his hands in his pockets. "He got such a charge out of meeting the players, and one thing kind of led to another."

"I know. I hear our team won."

"Yeah. Clipped them by one. I had to stop by the paper and file the story, or we'd have been here sooner."

"I just got in myself." On impulse, she walked over, wrapped her arms around him and hugged. Coop's hands stayed paralyzed in his pockets. "I owe you. You gave him a great day. He won't forget it." She drew back. "Neither will I."

"It's no big deal. He just hung out in the press box."

"It's a very big deal, especially since I trapped you into it." She laughed and tossed back her hair. "You were so transparent this morning, Coop. The idea of having a four-year-old tagging along terrified you. But you did good, real good. Anyway— Sorry," she said when the phone rang. "Hello? Oh, hi, Stan. Tonight? I'm not scheduled." Letting out a breath, she sat on the arm of a chair. "I'll have to let you know. No, Stan, I can't tell you now. I have to see if I can find a sitter. An hour, then. Yes, I understand you're in a jam. I'll call you back."

"Problem?"

"Hmmm… Two of the waitresses called in sick for tonight. They're short-staffed." She was already dialing the phone. "Hi, Mrs. Finkleman. Yeah, I know. He had a great time. Mm-hmm…" Zoe's gaze flicked up to Coop as Mrs. Finkleman told her how important it was for a boy to have a man in his life. "I'm sure you're right. I was wondering if you're busy tonight. Oh. That's right, I forgot. No, it's nothing. Have a good time."

Zoe hung up and pursed her lips. "It's their bingo night," she told Coop. "Beth's got a date. Maybe Alice." She reached for the phone again, shook her head. "No, she's having her in-laws over for dinner." Her eyes lit on Coop and narrowed in speculation. "You didn't have any problem with Keenan today."

"No," Coop said slowly, wary of another trap. "He was cool."

"Stan doesn't need me in until nine. Keenan goes to bed at eight, so you wouldn't have to do anything but hang around, watch television or whatever."

"Hang around here, while you work?" He took a step back. "Just me and the kid—like a baby-sitter? Listen…"

"I'll pay you. Beth gets two an hour, but I can up the ante."

"I don't want your money, Zoe."

"That's so sweet." She smiled, took his hand and squeezed. "Really, so sweet of you. If you could come down about eight-thirty."

"I never said—"

"You can help yourself to anything in the kitchen. I'll make some brownies, if I have time. I'd better call Stan back before he pulls out what's left of his hair." She picked up the phone, beamed at Coop. "Now I owe you two."

"Yeah, right." He hurried out before she could find some way to owe him three.

CHAPTER 5

For the next couple of hours, Coop immersed himself in "All in the Game," his weekly syndicated column. The kid had given him the hook, he thought. The first visit to a ball game, the passing on of tradition, and the bond that was forged over the cheers, the crack of the bat, the peanut shells.

It was a good piece, Coop decided, and wrote easily. He supposed since he owed the idea to Keenan the least he could do was hang around downstairs and eat brownies while the kid slept.

He wandered back down just as Zoe came through the kitchen door.

She hadn't been sure he'd come. She knew she'd hustled him, and after she'd finished being amused by it, she felt guilty. But here he was, right on time, standing at the foot of the steps.

"I pushed you into a corner...." she began.

"Yeah, you did." She looked so somber, he had to smile. "You've got a real talent for it."

She shrugged her shoulders and smiled back at him. "Sometimes being pushy's the only way to get things done, but I always feel bad about it after. I did bake brownies."

"I could smell them all the way upstairs." When she didn't move, he tilted his head. Funny, though she was wearing that sexy waitress rig again, she didn't seem so outrageous. Except for that bow tie, he thought. Something about that black tie around that slim white throat shot straight to his libido.

"You going to let me in, or do you want me to stand out here?"

"I have this guilt thing," she explained, "whenever I have to ask anyone for a favor. And it was so sweet of you to take Keenan to the game, especially when..."

"When I'd been asking you out?"

She shrugged her shoulders again, let them fall. He was looking at her that way again, and something in her body was reacting helplessly. Better, she thought, to set the rules quickly. "I don't go out with men. I should have told you straight out."

He had to force himself not to lift a hand to that neat little bow and tug. "At all?"

"It's just easier not to. They're not interested in

Keenan, or they pretend they are so they can talk me into bed." When he rocked back on his heels and cleared his throat, she laughed. "What they don't know is that they're clear as cellophane. You see, Keenan and I are a team. As a sportswriter, you should know what that means."

"Sure. I get it."

"Anyway, you gave him a really wonderful day, and I feel like I'm twisting your arm about tonight."

He decided, after a moment, that she wasn't doing it on purpose. There was just too much sincerity in that glorious face for a con. And if there was a twinge of guilt because he had given considerable thought to talking her into bed, that was his problem.

"Look, he's asleep, right?"

"Yes. All the excitement wore him out."

"So, I'll eat your brownies and watch your TV. No big deal."

Her smile came easily now, beautifully, and made his mouth water. "I left the number of the club by the phone, just in case. The Finklemans should be home by eleven. She'd come over and relieve you if you want."

"We'll play it by ear."

"Thanks, really." She stepped back into the kitchen to let him in. "My shift ends at two, at closing."

"Long day for you."

"I've got tomorrow off." After grabbing her purse, she took a quick look around. "Make yourself at home, okay?"

"I will. See you."

She hurried out, those incredibly sexy heels clicking across the tile. Coop let out a long breath and told himself to settle down. The lady had just set the ground rules. Fun and games were out.

She had the face of a siren, the body of a goddess, and legs designed to make a strong man whimper—but deep in her heart she was Betty Crocker.

Coop took a deep sniff and decided to content himself with a plate of double fudge brownies.

The storm rolled in just before midnight. Coop had taken Zoe at her word and made himself at home. He was stretched out on her couch, sunk deep in the cushions, with his feet propped comfortably on her coffee table. He was dozing in front of an old war movie, his only regret being that he hadn't thought to bring a couple of beers down with him.

Zoe's selection ran to milk, juice and some unidentified green liquid.

He'd poked around a little—it was simply in his nature. The clutter ran throughout the house, but he began to see a pattern to it. Obviously she wasn't a detail person, but the general lack of order made the house comfortable, even cozy. Coop wasn't sure if the result was by design or simply because she was a woman who worked two jobs and had a kid to raise.

And from the library books he'd found stacked here and there, it seemed she spent most of her free time reading up on flowers, car repair, tax laws and time management.

He couldn't help but think it was a waste of a perfectly stunning woman, this voluntary burial of self in books and nowhere part-time jobs.

But it wasn't his problem.

The crash of thunder from outside harmonized nicely with the artillery barrage on the TV screen. Coop had just decided that this baby-sitting racket was a snap.

Then he heard the wailing.

Marines didn't wail, he thought fuzzily, especially when they were battling Nazi scum. He yawned, circled his neck until it cracked, then spotted Keenan.

The boy stood at the base of the stairs in Batman pajamas, a battered stuffed dog clutched in one arm and tears pouring down his face.

"Mama!" His voice sharpened like an ice pick, then hitched. "Where's my mama?"

"She's at work." Coop straightened on the sofa and stared helplessly. "Something wrong?"

A flash of lightning lit the room. By the time the

thunder rolled in answer, Keenan screamed like a banshee and launched himself into Coop's lap.

"I'm scared. There's monsters outside. They're coming to get me."

"Hey…" Coop gave the head buried in his chest an inadequate pat. "Hey, it's just a thunderstorm."

"Monsters," Keenan sobbed. "I want Mama."

"Well, she's—" He started to swear, caught himself. The poor kid was shaking. With an instinct he didn't recognize, Coop cuddled Keenan in his lap. "You don't like storms, huh?" All Keenan could do was shake his head and burrow deeper. "They're just like fireworks. You know, on the Fourth of July, or after your team wins the pennant? They probably just had a big game up there. They're celebrating."

"Monsters," Keenan repeated, but he'd calmed enough to lift his head and look at Coop. "Big black monsters with sharp teeth." He jolted at the next clap of thunder. Fresh tears started to roll. "They want to eat me."

"Nah." Experimentally, Coop tested Keenan's biceps. "You're too tough."

"I am?"

"You bet. Any monsters who looked in here would see you and run for their lives. They'd never take on Coop and the Keen-man."

Keenan sniffled, rubbed a fist over his eyes. "Really?"

"Absolutely." Coop saw Keenan's lower lip tremble

when thunder grumbled. "Home run," he said, and Keenan's trembling mouth curved in a hesitant smile.

"Can I stay out here with you?"

"Sure. I guess."

Keenan, an expert in such matters, settled himself comfortably in Coop's lap, laid his head against Coop's heart and sighed.

Zoe was swaying with fatigue by the time she let herself in. It was nearly 3:00 a.m., and she'd been up and going for twenty hours straight. All she wanted was to fall facedown on her bed and sleep.

She saw them in the gray light of the snowy television screen. They were curled together on the couch, the boy snuggled deep against the man. Something shifted inside her at the sight of them, both sleeping deeply, Keenan's tousled golden hair beneath Coop's broad, tanned hand.

She set her purse and her keys aside without taking her eyes off them.

How small her son looked, and how safe.

She slipped out of her shoes and walked to them on stockinged feet. In a natural gesture, she brushed a hand over Coop's hair before gently lifting her son. Keenan stirred, then settled against her.

"Mama."

"Yes, baby," she murmured. She nuzzled him as she carried him away, caught the scent of man mixed with boy.

"The monsters came, but we scared them away."

"Of course you did."

"Coop said the thunder's just fireworks. I like fireworks."

"I know." She laid him in his bed, smoothing the sheets, his hair, kissing his soft cheeks. "Go back to sleep now."

But he already had. She watched him a moment longer in the faint glow of his night-light, then turned and went back downstairs to Coop.

He was sitting up now, his head in his hands, the heels rubbing against his eyes. She switched off the buzzing television set, then sat on the arm of the couch. Any man who could sleep so comfortably with a child, to her mind, had unlimited potential.

She wondered, just for an instant, what it would feel like to curl up beside him.

"The storm woke him?"

"Yeah." His voice was rusty. He cleared it. "He was pretty spooked."

"He said you chased the monsters away."

"Seemed like the right thing to do." He turned his head to look at her. Those big brown eyes were sleepy and smiling. The quick hitch in his heartbeat warned him to be on his way. But he lingered. "He's okay now?"

"He's fine. You'd make a good daddy."

"Oh, well…" That had him moving. He stood, working out the kinks. "That's not my line. But it was no big deal."

"It was to me." She'd embarrassed him, she noted, and she hadn't meant to. "Why don't I fix you breakfast tomorrow?"

"Huh?"

"Pay you back with pancakes. Mrs. Finkleman tells me you bring in a lot of pizza and Chinese, so I don't imagine you cook. Do you like pancakes?"

"Who doesn't?"

"Then let me know when you're up and around. I'll flip some for you." She lifted a hand, brushed the hair from his brow. "Thanks for helping me out."

"No problem." He took a step away, swore under his breath and turned back. "Listen, I've just got to do this, okay?"

Before she could respond, he took her face in his hands and closed his mouth over hers.

The kiss was quick, and it was light, and it sent sparks snapping down her nerve ends.

When she didn't move a muscle, he lifted his head, looked at her. She was staring at him, her eyes heavy and dark. He thought he saw the same stunned reaction in them that was curling somewhere in his gut. She opened her mouth as if to speak, but he shook his head and kissed her again. Longer, deeper, until he felt her bones begin to melt. Until he heard the small whimper of pleasure purr in her throat.

Her hands slid up his arms, gripped, then moved up to tangle in his hair. They stood there, locked against each other.

One of them quivered, perhaps both. It didn't seem to matter as the warm taste of her seeped into his mouth, into his blood. It was like a dream that he hadn't yet shaken off, one that tempted him to sink back in, to forget reality.

She'd forgotten it. All she knew for one glorious moment was that she was being held in strong arms, that her mouth was being savored wonderfully, and that needs, so long dormant, were swimming to the surface and breaking into life.

Touch me. She wondered if she said it, or if the words simply whirled hazily in her head. But his hand, hard and sure, ran once down her body, kindling fires.

She remembered what it was to burn, and what it was like when the flames died out and left you alone.

"Coop." Oh, she wanted, so badly, just to let it happen. But she wasn't a young, reckless girl this time. And she had more to think of than herself. "Coop. No."

His mouth clung to hers for another moment, his teeth nipping. But he drew back. He was, he realized, as breathless as a man who'd slid headfirst into home plate.

"Now I'm supposed to say I'm sorry."

She shook her head. "No, you're not. I'm not."

"Good." The hands that were resting on her shoulders kneaded once, then slipped away into his pockets. "Me neither. I've been thinking about doing that since I first saw your feet."

Her brows rose. Surely she'd heard him wrong. "My what?"

"Your feet. You were standing on the ladder, painting. You weren't wearing any shoes. You've got tremendously sexy feet."

"Really?" It amazed her that he could tie her into helpless knots one minute, then make her laugh the next. "Thanks. I think."

"I guess I'd better go."

"Yeah, you'd better."

He nodded, started out. This time, when he stopped, she braced, and she yearned. But he simply turned and looked at her. "I'm not going to try to talk you into bed. But I want you there. I figured I should let you know."

"I appreciate it," she said in a shaky voice.

When the door closed behind him, she let her weak legs fold and sat down on the couch. What, she asked herself, was she supposed to do now?

CHAPTER 6

When Coop dragged himself out of bed, it was nearly noon. He stumbled into the shower and nearly drowned himself before both of his eyes opened. Wet and out of sorts, he rubbed himself down, gave a moment's thought to shaving, then dismissed the idea.

He tugged on gym shorts and a T-shirt before heading directly to the coffeemaker. While it brewed, he opened his front door and let the full power of the sun shock him the rest of the way awake.

They were in the yard, Zoe and Keenan, laughing as mother tried to help son hit fungoes with a plastic bat. The kid wasn't having much luck, Coop noted. But he was sure having fun. He started to step back inside before either of them spotted him. But the jock in him had him kibitzing.

"He'll never hit anything standing that way," Coop

called out, and had two pairs of big brown eyes looking up in his direction.

"Hi, Coop. Hi. I'm playing baseball." Thrilled to
have an audience, Keenan waved his bat and nearly
caught his mother on the chin.

"Watch it, champ," she said, and shifted out of
range. "Good morning," she called out. "Want your
breakfast?"

"Yeah, maybe."

Keenan took another pathetic swing and had Coop
muttering under his breath. Swung like a girl. Somebody had to show the kid how to hold a bat, didn't they?
he asked himself as he started down.

"You're choking it too much."

Zoe's brows drew together. "The book I got said—"

"Book." He cursed automatically. Keenan echoed
him. "Sorry," he muttered when Zoe gave him a nar-
row-eyed look. "Now listen, you learn how to add and
subtract from books. You don't learn baseball. Just like
a girl." He crouched down and adjusted Keenan's hands.

Zoe had been ready to concede to the expert, but the
last statement stopped her. "Excuse me? Are you im-
plying that females can't play sports?"

"Not what I said. Swing from the shoulders," he told
Keenan. Coop might have been grouchy, but he wasn't
stupid. "There are plenty of terrific female athletes.
Keep your eye on the ball, kid." He kept one hand

around Keenan's and lightly tossed the ball up in the air with the other. The bat connected with a hollow thud.

"I hit it! I hit it really, really hard!"

"Major league stuff." Coop slid his eyes back up to Zoe's. "I thought you were making pancakes."

"I was— I am." She blew out a breath. "I guess you're taking over."

"Well, I don't know diddly about pancakes, and you don't know squat about baseball. Why don't we both do what we know?"

"Like it's a big deal to hit a stupid ball with a stupid bat," she muttered as she strode to the back door.

"You can't do it."

She stopped dead in her tracks, eyes narrowed, turned. "I certainly can."

"Yeah, right. Okay, Keenan, let's try it again."

"I believe it's my turn." Challenge in her every movement, Zoe slipped the bat from her son's hands.

"Are you going to hit it, Mama? Are you?"

"You bet I am." She held out a hand for the ball Coop was holding. She tossed it up, swung, and batted the ball to the chain-link fence bordering the side yard. Keenan let out a cheer and raced to retrieve it.

Coop sniffed, smiled. "Not bad, for a girl. But anybody can hit a fungo."

"Keenan's too young for anything but a plastic ball."

"No, a fungo's when you toss it up yourself and hit it."

"Oh."

"I'm gonna throw it, Coop. You catch."

"Sure, zip it in here."

It took Keenan three tries, running in closer each time, to send the ball anywhere near Coop.

"I suppose you don't think I could hit it if you threw it at me…." Zoe began.

"Pitch it to you," Coop said patiently. "I would pitch it to you."

"All right, pitch it to me, then." She raised the bat.

"Fine, but you might want to turn a little more to the side. That's it," he said, backing away. "Zoe, you're holding the bat like you're going to use it to hammer a nail. Okay, here it comes."

He tossed the ball soft and underhand, but she still had to grit her teeth to keep herself from jerking away. Because her pride and her son's respect for women were at stake, she swung hard. No one was more stunned than Zoe when she connected. Coop snatched the ball an instant before it could smash his nose.

"Well." Zoe handed the bat back to a wide-eyed Keenan, dusted her hands. "I'll go see about those pancakes."

"She hit it really hard," Keenan said admiringly.

"Yeah." Coop watched the back door swing shut behind her. "Your mother's really…something, kid."

"Will you pitch to me, Coop? Will you?"

"Sure. But let's work on that stance, huh? You gotta look like a ballplayer."

When Zoe finished flipping the last pancake on the stack, she looked out the window and saw her son swing the bat. The ball didn't go far, but Coop made a pretense of a diving catch, missing, while Keenan danced gleefully in place.

"Too hot to handle," Coop claimed, and Keenan jumped on top of him. "Hey, there's no tackling in baseball. Football's out of season." He scooped the wriggling boy up and held him upside down. Somewhere along the line, his sour mood had vanished.

It became a habit to spend time with the boy. Nothing planned, just playing a little catch in the yard or showing Keenan how to dunk baskets in the apartment. It wasn't as though he were attached to the kid, Coop assured himself. But when he had some free time and the boy wanted to hang around, what was the harm? Maybe it was sort of nice to see those big eyes all full of hero worship. And maybe it wasn't so much of a hardship to listen to that rollicking belly laugh Keenan burst into when something struck his fancy.

If the boy sometimes came along with the bonus of his mother, it wasn't exactly a hardship.

The fact was, he had seen a great deal more of Keenan than Zoe since the night of the thunderstorm.

She was friendly enough, but she'd been careful—or so it seemed to Coop—not to be alone with him.

That was something he was going to fix, he decided as he shut down his computer.

He grabbed a couple of miniature race cars, some of the flotsam and jetsam of boyhood that Keenan had left in his apartment. If Coop knew Zoe as he thought he was beginning to, the toys would be an easier entry than a bouquet of long-stemmed roses.

Jiggling the cars in his hand, he strode down the steps to knock on her kitchen door.

In the laundry room, Zoe slammed down the lid on the washer. "Who is it?"

"It's Coop."

She hesitated, started the machine. "Come on in. I'll be right out." She hefted a basket of clean laundry, as much out of defense as out of necessity, and went into the kitchen.

God, he looked good. She had really, really tried not to dwell on how good the man looked. So damn male, she thought, the rangy, athletic body, the muscles, the dark, untidy hair, and those wonderful pale green eyes. She wished her heart wouldn't always stutter when he aimed one of his cocky grins in her direction.

"Hi." She plopped the basket on the kitchen table and immediately began busying her hands folding socks.

"Hi." The kitchen was cluttered, as always. She really needed someone to help her organize, he thought. God, she smelled fantastic. "Keenan left these upstairs." Coop set the cars on the table. "I thought he might be looking for them."

"Thanks."

"So where is he?"

"In school."

"Oh, right." Coop knew Keenan's schedule as well as he knew yesterday's box scores. "You just get in from the flower shop?"

"Mmm-hmm… Business is picking up. We've got a couple of weddings. Actually, I could work full-time for the next three weeks, but it just doesn't fit Keenan's schedule."

"What do you mean?" Idly he plucked a shirt from the basket.

"Well, the spring weddings. The arrangements take a lot of extra hands, so Fred asked if I could put in full days for a while."

"So, that's good, right?"

"The school Keenan goes to is really more of a pre-school than day-care. It doesn't stay open after three. And I have the car pool next week, anyway. Plus, I promised to take him and some of the other kids swimming at the community center on Friday. He's really looking forward to it."

"Yeah, he mentioned it." About twenty times, Coop recalled.

"I don't want to let him down."

"So, I'll do it."

She looked back up, socks dangling from her hands. "What?"

He couldn't believe he'd said that. He stared at her for another moment, then shrugged. "I said I'd do it. It's no big deal. He can hang with me when he gets home from school."

She tilted her head. "Don't you have a job?"

"That's what I call it, since they pay me." He smiled, finding the idea went down easily. "I do most of my writing here, and he could tag along when I go in to the paper or on an interview. He'd probably get a kick out of it."

"I'm sure he would." She narrowed her eyes. Why couldn't she get a handle on J. Cooper McKinnon? "But why would you?"

He wasn't sure he had the answer to that, so he punted. "Why not? He's not that much of a pest."

With a laugh, she went back to her laundry. "Maybe he's not, but you forgot the car pool."

"I can drive. What's the big deal about hauling a bunch of kids to school and back?"

"I can't begin to tell you," she murmured. It was, perhaps, something every adult should experience for himself. "And the swimming."

"I was captain of the swim team in college. All-state."

She glanced up at that. "I thought you played baseball. Uh, Keenan mentioned it."

"Yeah, I did. Two hundred and twelve RBIs my last season. I played basketball, too, averaged forty-two points a game." He was bragging, Coop realized. Like some gawky teenager trying to impress the head cheerleader. He frowned down at the little cars, began to slide one over the table.

"Keenan says you make great engine noises."

"Yeah, it's a talent."

He'd embarrassed himself, Zoe realized, and she wanted to hug him. "Tell you what. Why don't we take it a day at a time? If you decide you can't handle it—"

His eyes flashed up at that. "I think I can handle one scrawny kid and a few of his pals."

"Okay. If you decide you don't *want* to handle it, no hard feelings."

"Fine. When do you want to start?"

"Tomorrow would be great."

"Okay." That was settled. Now, he thought, it was on to other business. "How about dinner?"

Her eyes widened in surprise. "Um…sure. We're just going to have chicken. I'll probably fry it."

"No." He stepped closer. She stepped back. "I mean, why don't we have dinner? Out. You and me."

"Oh, well…" Good answer, she thought foolishly. Very succinct. She took another step in retreat. "I have to work tonight."

"Tomorrow."

"I don't really go out."

"I've noticed. What are you backing away from, Zoe?"

"You." Annoyed with herself, she held up a hand. And found it pressed against his chest. "I don't want to date anyone. Start anything. I have very good reasons."

"You'll have to tell me about them sometime." He reached up, combed a hand through her hair and loosened the band that held it back.

"You're not going to kiss me again."

"Sure I am." He touched his lips to hers to prove it. His eyes remained open as he drew her lower lip into his mouth, as he used his tongue, his teeth, to tease and seduce. "You've got an incredible mouth."

She couldn't get her breath. Even as she gasped for it, her vision dimmed. It was all she wanted. It seemed her life depended on keeping her lips against his. This wasn't fair, she thought dimly as she began to sink into the glory of sensation. Too long, she told herself. Surely she was reacting this way only because it had been so terribly long since she'd allowed herself to feel only as a woman.

She was melting against him like wax. He hadn't known how painfully erotic it would be to feel that long, lean body go fluid. He'd only meant to kiss her, to test them both, but his hands were already reaching, stroking, exploring.

His touch, those hard, callused hands against her bare skin, all but brought her to her knees.

"I have to think."

"Think later." He pressed his mouth to her throat.

Oh, it was glorious, glorious to ache again. But she knew too well what came from soothing that ache. "Coop, we can't do this."

"Yes, we can. I'll show you."

With a laugh that came out half moan, she turned her head away. "My head's spinning. You have to stop. God, do you have any idea what you're doing to me?"

"I haven't even started. Come upstairs, come upstairs with me, Zoe. I want to feel you under me. I want to feel myself inside you."

"I want to." She trembled, the needs exploding inside her like firebombs. "Coop, I need to think first. I have to think. I haven't been with anyone in five years."

His mouth stopped its desperate journey over her throat. Slowly he drew back to look at her. Her eyes were clouded, and her mouth was swollen and ripe. "No one?"

"No." She swallowed and prayed for her system to level before she gave in to the urge to rip off his clothes and cut loose. "Since before Keenan was born. I feel like all those needs dried up—like old leaves. You've set a match to them, and I don't know how to handle it."

"The kid's father," Coop said carefully. "You're still in love with him."

"No." She might have laughed at that, if she weren't so shaken. "He has nothing to do with it. Well, of course he does, but... I have to sit down." She walked unsteadily to a chair. "I knew this was going to happen. I think I knew it the first time I saw you. There's been no one, because I didn't want anyone. Because Keenan was all that mattered to me. I have plans." That came out as an accusation, and her eyes darkened. "Damn it, I have plans. I want to go back to school. I want to have my own flower shop one day." Her voice began to catch, alarming him.

"Zoe—"

But she barreled right over him. "And everything was going along fine. I got the house. I wanted him to have a house, and a yard, and neighbors. Everyone said I was crazy, that I'd never be able to do it, that I'd be sorry I'd given everything up to raise a child on my own. But I'm not sorry. He's the best thing that ever happened to me. And I've done a good job. Keenan's happy, and he's bright and funny and wonderful. We have a good life, and I know I can make it even better. I haven't needed anyone. And... Oh, God, I'm in love with you."

The hand he'd lifted awkwardly to pat her head froze. "What?"

"Oh, what a mess. What a mess." She plucked a tiny sock out of the laundry basket and wiped her eyes. "Maybe it's just hormones. It could be, you know. But I walked in and you were sleeping with him on the couch. It was so sweet. Then you were kissing me and everything went crazy. Then you're out in the yard looking so smug and male, showing Keenan how to hit that silly ball. And you're eating pancakes and looking at me. I can hardly breathe when you're looking at me."

Somewhere along the line, his mind had gone blank. "I think I missed a step."

"No, you didn't." She sniffled and struggled to get herself under control. "I've just taken too many. It's my fault. You've been nice to Keenan, and you've been honest with me." She sighed, dropped the damp sock in her lap. "Believe me, I know my emotions are my responsibility." Because he was still staring at her, like a man who'd just had the friendly family dog lunge for his throat, she smiled. "I'm sorry, Coop. I shouldn't have dumped all that on you. I didn't even know it was all bottled up."

This time he took a step back. "Zoe, I like the kid. Who wouldn't? And I'm attracted to you. But—"

"There's no need to explain." Steady now, she rose. "Really, there isn't. I don't expect anything from you, and I'm sorry if I made you uncomfortable. But I feel a lot better." And, oddly enough, she did. "When I go to bed with you, we'll understand each other."

"When you—"

"I think we both know that's going to happen," she said calmly. "We both want it to, and it's smarter to face that than to live with all this tension. Keenan's been wanting to spend the night with a friend of his. I'll arrange it." She laughed a little at Coop's expression. "It's a little hard to be spontaneous with a four-year-old around. I hope you don't mind planning out a night together."

"No, I mean, I don't— God, Zoe."

"If you'd rather not, or if you want some time to decide, that's all right."

He studied her face, felt that same greedy tug, and a flare of something entirely different. Entirely new. "No, I want you. Whenever."

"How about Monday night?"

"I've got a twilight doubleheader on Monday." He couldn't believe he was standing here planning out a wild night of love like a dentist's appointment.

"Ah...Wednesday?"

He nodded. "Wednesday's good for me. Do you want to go out somewhere?"

It was sweet, she thought, really sweet of him to ask. "It's not necessary." She laid a hand on his cheek. "I don't need flowers and candlelight. I'll come upstairs after Keenan's settled."

"Good. Fine. I…better get back to work."

"Do you still want to have Keenan tomorrow?"

"Yeah, no problem. Tell him to come on up." Coop backed toward the door as Zoe began folding laundry again. "I guess I'll see you."

She listened to him walk up the steps. He was certainly a mistake, she told herself. But she'd made others. Life got too mundane when you avoided all the wrong turns.

CHAPTER 7

"He shoots, he scores!" Coop made appropriate crowd noises as Keenan dunked the basket.

"I can do it again! I can, okay?" From his perch on Coop's shoulders, Keenan swung his sneakered feet.

"Okay, you've drawn the foul." Coop scooped the palm-sized ball up and passed it into Keenan's eager hands. "It's game point, kid, ten seconds to play. This free throw is all-or-nothing. Got it?"

"Got it!"

"A hush falls over the crowd as Fleming steps up to the line. He's played the game of his life tonight, but it all comes down to this one shot. He eyes the basket. You eyeing the basket?"

"Eyeing it," Keenan said, with his tongue caught between his teeth.

"He sets...and shoots." Coop winced as the little rubber ball circled the rim, then watched through squinted eyes as it tipped in and dropped through the net.

"And the crowd goes wild!" Coop danced around the sofa while Keenan hooted and clapped on his shoulders. When he dumped the boy on the cushions of the sofa, Keenan let go with one of the rolling belly laughs that always made Coop grin. "You're a natural."

"You shoot it, Coop! You!"

Obliging, Coop executed a quick turnaround jump shot. This wasn't such a bad way to spend a rainy afternoon, he decided. And it helped keep his mind off how he was going to spend the rainy night ahead.

It was Wednesday.

"Okay, time out. I've got to finish up my piece on the track meet."

"Are we going to go to the paper again? It's neat there."

"Not today. I'm going to fax it in when it's done. You watch some tube." Coop hit the remote, then handed it over.

"Can I get a drink?"

"Yeah, there's some of that juice your mom sent up for you. Stay out of trouble, right?"

"Right."

When Coop headed into his office, Keenan scrambled up from the couch. He liked it best when he got to stay with Coop after school. They always got to do something neat, and Coop never asked if he'd washed his hands or said too many cookies would spoil his appetite.

Best of all, he liked when Coop picked him up. It was different than when his mother did. He liked when she held him, nuzzled him after his bath or rocked him when he had a bad dream. But Coop smelled different, and felt different.

He knew why, Keenan thought as he wandered into the kitchen. It was because Coop was a daddy instead of a mom.

He liked to pretend Coop was his daddy, and figured that maybe if he didn't do anything bad, Coop wouldn't go away.

After a couple of tugs, Keenan had the refrigerator open. He was proud that Coop had hung the pictures he had drawn for him on the door. He peered inside, saw the jug of juice his mother had bought for him. And the green bottles Coop liked.

"B-E-E-R," Keenan said to himself. He remembered that he'd asked Coop if he could have a taste from the bottle, and that Coop had told him he couldn't until he was big. After Coop had let him sniff the beer, Keenan had been glad he wasn't big yet.

There was a new bottle in the fridge today, and Keenan knit his brow and tried to recognize the letters. C-H-A-R-D-O-N— There were too many letters to read, so he lost interest.

He took out the jug, gripping it manfully and setting it on the floor. Humming to himself, he dragged a
chair over to get cups from the cabinet. One day he'd
be as tall as Coop and wouldn't need to stand on a chair.
He leaned forward on his toes.

The crash and the howl had Coop leaping up, rap-
ping his knee hard against the desk. Papers scattered as
he raced out of the office and into the kitchen.

Keenan was still howling. A chair was overturned,
juice was glugging cheerfully onto the floor, and the refrigerator was wide open. Coop splashed through the
puddle and scooped Keenan up.

"Are you hurt? What'd you do?" When his only answer was another sob, he stood Keenan on the kitchen
table and searched for blood. He imagined gaping
wounds, broken bones.

"I fell down." Keenan wriggled back into Coop's arms.

"Okay, it's okay. Did you hit your head?"

"Nuh-uh." With a sniffle, Keenan waited for the
kisses he expected after a hurt. "I fell on my bottom."
Keenan's lip poked out. "Kiss it."

"You want me to kiss your— Come on, kid, you're
joking."

The lip trembled, another tear fell. "You gotta kiss
where it hurts. You gotta, or it won't get better."

"Oh, man." Flummoxed, Coop dragged a hand
through his hair. He was desperately relieved that no

blood had been spilled, but if anyone, anyone, found out what he was about to do, he'd never live it down. He turned Keenan around and made a kissing noise in the air. "Does that do it?"

"Uh-huh." Keenan knuckled his eyes, then held out his arms. "Will you pick me up?"

"Yeah." He didn't feel as ridiculous as he'd expected when the boy's arms went around his neck. "Okay now?"

With his head resting on Coop's shoulder, he nodded. "I didn't mean to do it. I spilled all the juice."

"No big deal." Hardly realizing he did so, Coop turned his head to brush his lips over Keenan's hair. Something was shifting inside him, creaking open.

"You aren't mad at me? You won't go away?"

"No." What the hell was going on? Coop wondered as unexplored and unexpected emotions swirled inside him. "No, I'm not going anywhere."

"I love you," Keenan said, with the simple ease of a child.

Coop closed his eyes and wondered how a grown man was supposed to handle falling for a four-year-old boy.

Well, here she was, Zoe thought as she stood at the bottom of the steps leading to Coop's apartment. All she had to do was go upstairs, open the door and start an affair. Her stomach clenched.

Silly to be nervous, she told herself, and climbed the

first step. She was a normal woman with normal needs. If her emotions were too close to the surface, she would deal with it. It was much more difficult to be hurt when you had no expectations.

She'd had expectations once, but she knew better now.

This was simply a physical attraction between two single, healthy people. She'd nearly backed down a step before she forced herself to move forward. All the practical details had been seen to. Her son was safely tucked away for the night at his sleep-over. She'd arranged for birth control—that wasn't an oversight she would make again.

No regrets, she promised herself as she lifted a hand to knock. She knew how useless they were.

He answered so quickly, she nearly jumped. Then they stood and stared at each other.

She'd worn a dress, one of those thin, breezy sundresses designed to make a man give thanks for the end of winter. Her hair was loose, falling over thin raspberry-colored straps and bare, peach-toned shoulders. There were nerves in her eyes.

"Hi." He glanced down to the cordless phone she held. "Expecting a call?"

"What? Oh." She laughed, miserably self-conscious. "No, I just don't like to be out of touch when Keenan's not home."

"He's all settled at his pal's?"

"Yeah." She stepped inside, set the phone on the

counter. "He was so excited, he—" She broke off when her sandal stuck to the floor.

Coop grimaced. "I guess I missed some of it. We had a spill."

"Oh?"

"The kid took a tumble, sheared off ten years of my life. No blood lost, though. Just a half gallon of orange juice." When she only smiled, he stepped to the refrigerator. Why in hell was he babbling? "Want some wine?"

"That would be nice." Why, he's as nervous as I am, she realized, and she loved him for it. "Keenan's having a wonderful time staying with you. I have to study the sports pages now just to keep up with what he's talking about."

"He catches on fast."

"So do I. Go ahead," she said as he handed her a glass of wine, "Ask me about stats. I know all about RBIs and ERAs." She took a sip, then gestured with her glass. "I think the Orioles would have taken the second game of that doubleheader the other night if they'd put in a relief pitcher in the second inning."

His lips twitched. "Do you?"

"Well, the starter had lost his stuff, obviously. The guy who was announcing—"

"The play-by-play man."

"Yes, he said so himself."

"So, you watched the game."

"I watch 'Sesame Street,' too. I like to keep up with Keenan's interests." She trailed off when Coop reached out to twine a lock of her hair around his finger.

"He's got a thing for dinosaurs, too."

"I know, I've checked a half dozen books out of the library. We've—" The fingers trailed over her shoulder. "We've been down to the natural history museum twice."

She set the glass aside and fell into his arms.

He kissed her as though he'd been starved for her taste. The impact was fast, deep, desperate. The little purring sounds that vibrated in her throat had his muscles turning into bundles of taut wire.

"I wasn't sure you'd come."

"Neither was I. I—"

"Can't think of anything but you," he said as he swept her off her feet. "I thought we'd take this slow."

"Let's not," she murmured, pressing her lips to his throat as he carried her into the bedroom.

She had a quick impression of Spartan neatness and simple masculine colors and lines before they tumbled onto the bed.

Neither of them was looking for patience. They rolled together, a tangle of limbs grasping, groping, glorying. The sheer physicality of it, flesh to flesh, mouth to mouth, had Zoe's head reeling. Oh, she wanted to be touched like this, to feel so desperately like a woman, with a man's hand streaking over her, with his lips savoring every thud of her pulse.

So she lost herself. No more nerves, no more fears. And if she loved, it only made the joy of mating more lovely.

She was every man's fantasy. Stunningly responsive, breathlessly aggressive. And so beautiful, he thought. Undraped, the exquisite body was so slim, so perfect, he couldn't believe it had ever carried a child. In the gilded light of dusk, her face was elegant, heart-stopping. Whenever he touched, wherever he touched, he could see the bold echo of her pleasure reflected in her eyes.

He watched those eyes glaze over, felt her body tense, heard her strangled cry of release. Swamped with the power of it, he drove her upward again until they were both panting for air, until she reared up from the bed and wrapped herself around him.

Damp skin slid over damp skin, hungry mouth sought hungry mouth. They rolled over the bed again, moaning, quivering. Then his hands gripped hers, and his mouth crushed her mouth. And he thrust inside her, hard and deep.

She felt the sensation as if it were a lance through her system, painful, glorious. For an instant, neither of them moved, they just stayed tensed and shuddering on the edge.

Then it was all movement, all speed, a wild race that ended with them both plunging deliriously over the finish line.

It wasn't exactly the way he'd imagined, Coop thought. They were sprawled across his bed, Zoe curled against him. The light was nearly gone, and the room was full of shadows.

He'd imagined they would progress to the bedroom by stages. They were both adults and had known that was the ultimate goal, but he'd thought they would move slowly.

Then she'd been standing there smiling, the nerves shining in her eyes… He'd never wanted anything or anyone more in his life.

Still, he thought she deserved more than a quick tussle, however rewarding. But the night was young.

He flexed his arm to bring her head a little closer, brushed his lips over her temple. "Okay?"

"Mmm… At the very least." Her body felt golden. She was surprised her skin didn't glow in the dark.

"I rushed you a little."

"No, perfect timing."

He began to trail a finger up and down her arm. He wanted her again. Good God, his system was already churning to life. A little control, Coop, he ordered himself. "You're going to stay?"

She opened her eyes, looking into his. "Yes."

"I'm going to go get the wine."

"That's good." She sighed as he left the bed. She'd forgotten how to deal with the after, she realized. Or with the before and during, for that matter, she thought with a wry smile. Though she thought she'd done pretty well so far.

She hadn't known how much had been bottled up inside her. Or just how much she'd needed to feel like a woman again. But then, she hadn't known she could love again.

She shifted, slipping under the tangled sheets, automatically lifting them to her breasts when Coop came back with the wine and glasses.

The sight of her in his bed shot to his loins, with a quick detour through the heart. He said nothing, pouring wine, offering her a fresh glass and settling beside her.

"Why haven't you been with anyone?" The moment the question was out, he wished for a rusty knife to hack off his tongue. "Sorry, none of my business."

"It's all right." Because I haven't fallen in love with anyone before you, she thought. But that wasn't what he wanted to hear, she knew. Nor was it really what he'd asked.

"You want to know about Keenan's father."

"None of my business," he repeated. "Sorry, it's the reporter in me."

"It was a long time ago—a lifetime ago. I don't mind telling you. I grew up in New York. I think I mentioned that my mother's an actress. I was the result of a second marriage. She's had five. So far."

"Five?"

Zoe chuckled into her wine, sipped. "Clarice falls in love and changes husbands the way some women change hairstyles. My father lasted about four years before they parted amicably. Clarice always has friendly divorces. I didn't see much of him, because he moved to Hollywood. He does commercials and voice-overs mostly. Anyway, I think she was on husband number four when I was in high school. He had some pull with the Towers Modeling Agency. They're pretty big."

"I've heard of them."

"Well, he got me in. I started doing some shoots. And I caught on."

"That's it," Coop said, interrupting her. "I knew I'd seen your face before."

She moved her shoulders. "Five, six years ago, it was hard to avoid it. I did twenty covers in one month, the year after I graduated school."

"Cover of *In Sports,* swimsuit edition."

She smiled. "You've got a good memory. That was six years ago."

He remembered the long, sand-dusted legs, the lush

wet red excuse for a bathing suit, the laughing, seductive face. He gulped down wine. "It was a hell of a shot."

"And a long, grueling shoot. Anyway, I was making
a lot of money, getting a lot of press, going to lots of
parties. I met Roberto at one of them."

"Roberto." Coop grimaced at the sound of the
name.

"Lorenzi. Tennis player. You might have heard of
him."

"Lorenzi? Sure—took the French Open three years
ago in straight sets, then blew Wimbledon in the semis.
He's got a bad attitude and likes to race cars and chase
women on the side. Hasn't been seeded above twenty-
fifth in the last two years. Got some bad press this spring
when he tipped back too many vinos and punched out
a photographer." Coop started to drink, stopped.
"Lorenzi? He's Keenan's father? But he's—"

"A womanizer?" Zoe supplied. "A creep, a rich, spoiled
egotist? I know—now. What I saw then was a gorgeous,
charming man who sent me roses and jetted me off to
Monte Carlo for intimate dinners. I was dazzled. He told
me he loved me, that he adored me, worshiped me, he
couldn't live without me. I believed him, and we became
lovers. I thought, since he was my first, he'd be my only.
Anyway, I didn't realize he was already getting tired of
me when I found out I was pregnant. When I told him,
he was angry, then he was very calm, very reasonable. He

assumed I'd want an abortion and agreed to pay all the expenses, even to make the arrangements."

"A real prince."

"It was a logical assumption," Zoe said calmly. "I had a career on fast forward, in a field that wouldn't wait while I put on weight and suffered from morning sickness. He, of course, had no intention of marrying me, and thought, rightly enough, that I knew the rules of the game. I did know them," she said quietly. "But something had changed when the doctor confirmed the pregnancy. After the disbelief, the panic, even the anger, I felt good. I felt right. I wanted the baby, so I quit my job, moved away from New York and read everything I could get my hands on about parenting."

"Just like that?"

"Well, there were some scenes, some dire predictions, and a lot of anger, but that's how it worked. Roberto and I parted less than amicably, but with the agreement that he would stay out of my life and I would stay out of his."

"What have you told Keenan?"

"It's tough." And it never failed to make her feel guilty. "So far I've just told him his father had to go away, that he wasn't going to come back. He's happy, so he doesn't ask a lot of questions."

"Are you? Happy?"

"Yes." She smiled and touched his cheek. "I am. All my life I wanted a home, a family, something solid and settled. I didn't even know it until Keenan. He changed my life."

"No urge to go back and smile for the camera?"

"Oh, no. Not even a twinge."

He cupped a hand behind her neck, studying her. "It's such a face," he murmured. Right now he liked the idea of having it all to himself.

CHAPTER 8

The concept of car pools obviously had been devised by someone with a foul and vicious sense of humor. Having lived most of his life in cities where public transportation or a quick jog would get a man from his home to his office, Coop had never experienced the adult version.

But he'd heard rumors.

Arguments, petty feuds, crowded conditions, spilled coffee.

After a week as designated driver, Coop had no doubt the kiddie version was worse. Infinitely worse.

"He's pinching me again, Mr. McKinnon. Brad's pinching me."

"Cut it out, Brad."

"Carly's looking at me. I told her to stop looking at me."

"Carly, don't look at Brad."

"I'm going to be sick. Mr. McKinnon, I'm going to be sick right now."

"No, you're not."

Though Matthew Finney made gagging noises that had the other kids screeching, Coop gritted his teeth and kept driving. Matt threatened to be sick twice a day unless he rode in the front seat. After five miserable days Coop had his number. But that did very little to soothe his nerves.

Keenan, who had waited all week for his turn in the front, swiveled in his seat to make monster faces at Matt. This incited a small riot of elbow jabs, howls, screaming giggles and shoves.

"Keenan, turn around!" Coop snapped. "You guys straighten up back there. Cut it out! If I have to stop this car…" He trailed off, shuddered. He'd sounded like his own mother. Now Coop was afraid *he* would be sick. "Okay, first stop. Matt, scram."

Fifteen minutes later, his back seat thankfully empty, Coop pulled into the drive and rested his throbbing head on the steering wheel. "I need a drink."

"We got lemonade," Keenan told him.

"Great." He reached over to unbuckle Keenan's seat belt. All he needed was a pint of vodka to go with it.

"Can we go swimming again soon?"

The idea of taking a herd of screaming kids back to the community pool anytime within the next century had a stone lodging in Coop's heart. "Ask your mother."

Coop started to look in the back seat and realized he couldn't face it. Earlier in the week he'd made that mistake, and discovered wads of chewing gum on the rug, cookie crumbs everywhere, and a mysterious green substance smeared on the seat.

In his weakened state, even a candy wrapper was likely to tip the balance.

"Yoo-hoo!" Mrs. Finkleman stripped off her flowered garden gloves and headed across the lawn in a flowing tent dress and electric-blue sandals. "How was your swim, little man?"

"We had races, and Brad dunked Carly and made her cry even though Coop told him not to, and I can hold my breath underwater for twelve seconds."

"My goodness." She laughed and ruffled Keenan's hair. "You'll be in the Olympics next." Her shrewd eyes took in Coop's haggard face. "You look a little frazzled, Coop. Keenan, why don't you run in and tell Mr. Finkleman you want a piece of that cherry cobbler he baked today?"

"Okay!" He tugged on Coop's hand. "Do you want some? Do you wanna come?"

"I'll pass. You go ahead."

Mrs. Finkleman chuckled as Keenan darted away and scrambled up the steps. "Little angel. We'll keep him entertained for a couple of hours—or he'll keep us entertained. You look like you could use a few minutes in a quiet room."

"Padded room," Coop muttered. "How does anyone survive kids?"

"It's easier if you go through the stages with them. Once you've walked the floor all night with a colicky baby, nothing much fazes you." She sighed. "Except science projects. Science projects always took me to the edge. And that first driving lesson." She shook her head at the memory. "That can bring you to your knees." She beamed and patted his arm. "But there's years yet to worry about that. And you've been doing a fine job. Why, Harry and I were just saying how nice it is that Zoe and Keenan have a man in their lives. Not that Zoe hasn't been handling everything. Raising that sweet-natured boy all alone, and working two jobs and tending the house. But it does my heart good to see you and that little angel playing ball in the yard, or the way Zoe lights up when you're around. You make a lovely little family. Now, you go and take a nice nap. We'll keep an eye on your boy."

"I'm not— He's not—" But even as Coop stammered, she was drifting away.

Family? he thought as a ball of ice formed in his stomach. They weren't a family. Oh, no, he promised himself as he walked around the house to his steps. He hadn't taken that on.

He liked the kid, sure. What wasn't to like? And he was damn near nuts about the mother. But that didn't make them a family. That didn't make things permanent. Maybe he'd volunteered to spend time with the kid, taught him a few things about ball, pitched him a few, but that didn't make him Daddy.

He headed straight for the refrigerator, popped the top off a beer and took a long pull.

Sure, maybe he enjoyed having the kid around, and Lord knows he enjoyed being with Zoe. He'd even been sort of pleased when a woman at the pool mistook Keenan for his and commented on what a handsome son he had. But that didn't mean he was going to start thinking about family health insurance or college funds.

He was single. He liked being single. It meant coming and going as he pleased, planning all-night poker games, spending all day with the sports channel blaring.

He liked working in his own space—that was why he did the bulk of his writing at home, rather than at the paper. He didn't like people messing with his things or structuring his time or planning outings.

Family life—as he remembered from his childhood—was lousy with outings.

No way was he changing his nice comfortable existence to accommodate a family.

So he'd made a mistake, Coop decided, and stretched out on the couch with his beer. He'd given Zoe and the kid a little too much of his time, a little too much of his attention. It hadn't been anything he didn't want to give, but he could see now that the gesture could be misconstrued. Particularly since Zoe had once brought up the *L* word. Only once, he reminded himself, and he'd like to think that had just been a woman thing.

Still, if he didn't back off, they might start to depend on him. He shifted uncomfortably as the idea flitted through his mind that he might also come to depend on them.

It was time to reestablish himself as the tenant upstairs.

Keenan raced out of the house next door the minute his mother pulled her car in the drive.

"Hi, Mama, hi! I held my breath for twelve seconds underwater!"

Zoe caught him on the fly and swung him twice. "You must be hiding gills in there," she said, tickling his ribs. "Hi, Mrs. Finkleman."

"Hi yourself. We've had ourselves a fine hour. I sent Coop up for a nap when they got home. He looked like he'd had a rough day."

"Thanks." She kissed Keenan's waiting lips, then smacked her own. "Mmm... Cherries."

"Mr. Finkleman baked them, and they were good."

"I bet. Did you say thank you?"

"Uh-huh. Matt almost throwed up in Coop's car."

"Threw up," Zoe said as she carried Keenan inside.

"Uh-huh. 'Cause it was my turn to ride in the front. I had the best time, and Coop helped me to swim without my bubbles. He said I was a champ."

"That's just what you are." She collapsed with him on a chair. The idea of fixing dinner, changing into her uniform and serving drinks for six hours loomed heavily. "Give me a hug," she demanded, then soothed herself with some nuzzling. "Definitely a champion hugger. Why don't you come in the kitchen and tell me what else you did today while I fix dinner?"

A half hour later, as Zoe was draining pasta and Keenan was entertaining himself with crayons and paper on the kitchen floor, she heard the sound of Coop's feet on the stairs. Her heart sped up. The normal, healthy reaction made her smile. Imagine, she thought, believing herself immune to men.

She left the pasta draining in the sink and went to the back door just as he came to the foot of the steps.

"Hi."

"How's it going?" Coop jingled the keys in his pocket. Did she look all lit up? he wondered. She was smiling, and despite the shadows of fatigue under them, her eyes did have the prettiest lights in them.

"I was just going to call upstairs. I thought you'd like some dinner after a hard day at the pool." She opened the screen door and leaned out to kiss him. The smile dimmed a bit when he eased back. "It's just chicken and pasta."

It smelled nearly as good as she did. He glanced inside—the homey scene, cluttered counters, fresh flowers, steam rising from a pan on the stove, the child sprawled on the floor, the pretty woman offering him food and kisses.

A definite trap.

"Thanks, but I'm on my way out."

"Oh. I thought you had a couple hours before game time." She laughed at his arched brow. "I guess I've been paying more attention to the sports scene. Baltimore versus Toronto, game one of three."

"Yeah." When she starts to take an interest in *your* interests, she's really shutting the cage door. "I've got some stuff to do."

"Can I go with you?" Keenan dashed to the door to tug on Coop's slacks. "Can I go to the game? I like watching them with you best."

Coop could almost hear the locks clicking into place. "I've got too much to do," he said, with an edge to his voice that had Keenan's lips quivering. "Look, it's not just a game, it's my job."

"You said I was good luck."

"Keenan." Zoe put her hand on her son's shoulder to draw him back, but her eyes stayed on Coop's. "Did you forget Beth was coming over to stay with you tonight? She'll be here soon, and you're going to watch a tape of your favorite movie."

"But I wanna—"

"Now go wash your hands for dinner."

"But—"

"Go on now."

The way Keenan's face crumpled would have softened an ogre's heart. Dragging his feet, he headed out of the kitchen.

"I can't take him with me everywhere...." Coop began defensively.

"Of course not. He's just overtired. I couldn't have let him go, in any case." She hesitated, wishing she could ignore her instincts. "Is everything all right?"

"Everything's fine." He didn't know why he shouted it. He didn't know why he felt like something slimy stuck to the bottom of a shoe. "I have a life, you know. I don't need kids climbing up my back or you fixing me dinner. And I don't have to explain myself."

Her eyes turned very cool, her face very composed. "You certainly don't. I appreciate you helping me out the past couple of weeks. Let me know if I can return the favor."

"Look, Zoe—"

"I've got to get dinner on the table, or I'll be late for work." She let the screen door slam between them. "Enjoy the game."

She knew exactly how long he continued to stand

there while she worked at the stove. Knew exactly when he turned and walked away.

It wasn't unexpected, she reminded herself. This backing away was typical, even understandable. Perhaps it had taken Coop a few weeks to completely comprehend that she didn't come as a single. She was part of a pair, a ready-made family, with its share of responsibilities and problems and routines.

And he was opting out.

He might not even know it yet, she thought, but he was in the first stages of a full retreat.

Her eyes blurred, her chest heaved. Resolutely she choked the tears back. She would indulge herself with a nice long cry later, she promised. But for now she had a little boy to soothe.

When he came back in, she crouched down until they were eye-to-eye.

"You had a good time with Coop today, didn't you?"

Keenan sniffled, nodded.

"And he's taken you a lot of places. You've had fun, and done a lot of new things."

"I know."

"You should be grateful for that, baby, instead of pouting because you can't have more."

She straightened again and hoped she could take her own advice.

CHAPTER 9

"**Y**ou're spending a lot of time around here." Ben edged a hip onto the corner of Coop's desk. All around Coop's cubicle phones rang, keyboards clattered.

"So?" Without taking his eyes from the computer screen, Coop hammered out the draft of his weekly column.

"I just figured you had it made in that apartment of yours. I mean, great location." He thought of Zoe. "Great view. You didn't spend as much time in here when you lived downtown."

"I needed a change of scene."

"Yeah." Ben snorted and picked up a baseball from Coop's desk. "Trouble in paradise?"

"I don't know what you're talking about. And I've got a column to write."

"Pretty obvious the last few weeks that you've been

stuck on the landlady." He tossed the ball from one hand to the other. "I mean, when a man hauls a kid around, buys little baseball jerseys, it follows that he's hooking a line into Mom."

Coop's eyes flashed up. "I like the kid, okay? I don't have to use a four-year-old to get a woman. The kid's cool."

"Hey, I got nothing against rug rats. Might even have a few of my own one day. The thing is, when a woman's got one, a man has to play Daddy if he wants the inside track."

"Who says I have to play at anything to get a woman?"

"Not me. But it was you who couldn't shoot hoop last week because you were taking the family to the aquarium." Ben winked, set the ball down. "Still, I bet you scored better than I did." Ben jerked back as Coop lunged for his throat.

"It's not like that," Coop said between his teeth.

"Hey, hey. Just yanking your chain. I wouldn't have made any cracks if I'd known you were serious about her."

Coop's grip loosened. "I didn't say I was serious. I said it wasn't like that."

"Whatever you say."

Disgusted with himself, Coop dropped back in his chair. He and Ben had been riding each other about women for better than five years. No reason to overreact, he thought. Or to make a fool of himself. "Sorry. I've got a lot on my mind."

"Forget it. What you need's a distraction. You coming to the poker game tonight?"

"Yeah."

"Good. Losing money should put you back on track."

Something had to, Coop thought as he sat back alone in his cubicle to stare at his screen. For the past three days he'd slept little, eaten less, and gone around in a constant state of flux.

Because he was avoiding the issue, he decided. Opting to bunt, when he should be swinging away. The only solution to getting his life back in order was to face the problem head-on.

He flicked off his terminal.

The beautiful thing about an afternoon off, Zoe thought, was the solitude. No customers to talk to, no orders to fill. It meant she didn't have to be salesclerk, or waitress, or Mom, or anything but Zoe.

Sitting on the back stoop, she struggled to understand the assembly instructions for the new barbecue grill she'd bought. She was going to surprise Keenan with hamburgers.

She liked the quiet—her kind of quiet, which meant there was music throbbing from the kitchen radio. She liked the loneliness—her kind of loneliness, which meant Keenan would dash toward her shortly with open arms and chattering voice.

She knew the upstairs apartment was empty, and she tried not to think about that. Tried not to think about the fact that Coop had been away more than he'd been home in the last few days.

Foolish of her to have thought he was different. He'd wanted her, he'd had her, and now he'd lost interest. Well, she had wanted him, so they were even there. If her heart was suffering it would pass. It had passed before. She and Keenan could get along fine on their own. Just like always.

Her screwdriver slipped, scraped her knuckles, had her swearing.

"What the hell are you doing?"

Eyes hot, she looked up at Coop. "Baking a cake. What does it look like I'm doing?"

"You can't put something together if you're going to spread parts all over the damn place." Automatically he bent down to organize. She rapped his hand away with the rubber grip of the screwdriver.

"I don't need you to put things together for me. I'm not some poor helpless female who needs a man to pick up the slack. I managed just fine before you came along."

Stung, he rammed his hands in his pockets. "Fine. Do it yourself."

"I am doing it myself. I like doing it myself."

"Terrific. And when the thing topples over, you won't have anyone else to blame."

"That's right." She blew her hair out of her eyes. "I accept when something's my fault." She picked up a wrench and locked a bolt in place. "Do you plan to hover over me all afternoon?"

"I want to talk to you."

"So talk."

He had it well planned. He was a writer, after all. "I realize the way I've been hanging around with you and the kid—"

"His name is Keenan," Zoe said between her teeth.

"I know what his name is. The way I've been hanging around the last few weeks might give the wrong impression."

"Oh, really?" She looked up again, tapping the wrench against her palm.

"He's a great kid, he kind of grows on you. I've gotten a kick out of spending time with him."

Though she hated herself for it, Zoe softened. She understood that he was genuinely fond of Keenan. That only made it all the more difficult. "He likes spending time with you. It's been good for him."

"Well, yeah, on the one hand. On the other, I started thinking that he—that you—that both of you might get the wrong idea. I mean, tossing a ball around or taking him to a game, that's cool. I just don't want him thinking it's like—permanent."

"I see." She was calm now, frigidly so. It would help keep the hurt in check. "You're afraid he might begin to see you as a father figure."

"Well, yeah. Kind of."

"That's natural enough. But then, he spends a lot of time with Mr. Finkleman, too, and with Billy Bowers down the street."

"Finkleman's old enough to be his grandfather, and the Bowers kid is eighteen." Coop backed off, realizing there was a touch of jealousy in the defense. "And they don't have the same sort of thing going with you."

She arched both brows. "Thing?"

"Relationship," he said tightly. "Whatever the hell you want to call it. Damn it, we only slept together once."

"I'm aware of that." Carefully she set the wrench aside. It would give her only momentary pleasure to heave it at his head.

"That came out wrong," he said, furious with himself. "It sounded like it didn't mean anything. It did, Zoe." A great deal, he was afraid. A very great deal. "It's just that…"

"Now you're terrified that Keenan and I will trap you into a family. That you'll wake up one morning and be Daddy, with a wife and a mortgage and a small boy who needs attention."

"Yes. No. Something like that." He was burying himself, he realized, and he suddenly didn't know why. "I just want to make myself clear."

"Oh, I think you have. Perfectly." She rubbed her hands on her knees as she studied him. "You needn't worry, Coop. I advertised for a tenant, not a father for my child, or a husband for myself. I slept with you because I wanted to, not because I thought I could lure you to the altar."

"I didn't mean it like that." Frustrated, he dragged a hand through his hair. However well he'd planned this little scene, it was going all wrong. "I wanted you. I still do. But I know how badly you were let down before. I don't want to hurt you, Zoe. Or the kid. I just don't want you thinking I'd slide into the gap."

The anger came back, one swift wave of it that reddened her vision. She was on her feet before either of them realized she'd moved. "Keenan and I don't have a gap. We're a family, as real and as complete and as full a family as any could be." She jabbed the wrench at his chest. "Just because Daddy doesn't make three doesn't mean we're less of a unit."

"I didn't mean—"

"I'll tell you what you mean. You see a woman and a small boy and you think they're just pining away for some big strong man to come along and fulfill them. Well, that's bull. If I needed a man, I'd have one. And if I thought Keenan needed a father to make him happy,

I'd find him one. And," she continued, advancing and giving him another jab, "if you think you're at the head of some fictional list, you're wrong. Maybe I'm in love with you, but that's not enough. It's not just me, and it's not just you. Keenan comes first. When and if I want a father for Keenan, he'll be someone with compassion and patience, someone willing to adjust his life to make room for my son. So relax, Cooper. You're in the clear."

"I didn't come here to fight with you."

"Good, because I'm finished."

He grabbed her arm before she could turn away. "I haven't. I'm trying to be straight with you, Zoe. I care about you, okay? About both of you. I just don't want it to get out of hand."

"Out of whose hands?" she retorted. "Yours? Then that's no problem, is it? Because you know how to hold on to everything inside, really tight. Just keep holding on to it, Coop. Don't worry about me or about Keenan. We'll be fine." She jerked her arm free and sat again. Picking up the instruction sheet, she gave it her full attention.

Now why, he wondered, did he feel as though he'd just been rejected? Shaking his head, Coop took a step in retreat. "As long as we're clear."

"We are."

"I've, ah, got a little time, if you want me to help you put that grill together."

"No thanks. I can do it." She slanted him a look. "I'm

going to grill burgers later. You're welcome to join us. Unless you're afraid it will lead to a commitment."

She shoots, he thought wryly, she scores. "Thanks anyway. I've got plans. Maybe I could take a rain check."

"Fine. You know where to find us."

He got drunk. Not sloppily, but thoroughly. When Coop poured himself out of the cab and staggered toward the house, he already knew he'd hate himself in the morning. But it was tonight he had to deal with.

He leaned heavily against Zoe's front door and waited for the porch to settle down under his feet. She might think they'd finished, he told himself blearily, but she was wrong. Dead wrong.

He'd thought of a dozen things he had to say to her. There was no time like the present.

Lifting a fist, he pounded on the door. "Come on, Zoe." He pounded again. "I know you're in there." He saw a light flick on inside and kept on pounding. "Come on, come on. Open up."

"Coop?" From the other side of the door, Zoe belted her hastily donned robe. She'd been home from the lounge for barely twenty minutes, and in bed for less than five. "It's after two o'clock in the morning. What do you want?"

"I want to talk to you. Let me in."

"We'll talk in the morning."

"You just said it was morning."

When he pounded again, she flicked off the locks. "Stop that—you'll wake Keenan." Furious, she yanked open the door and had the surprise of a hundred-and-seventy-pound male tumbling against her. "Are you hurt? What happened?" The alarm signals that had screamed on shifted when she caught the scent of beer. "You're drunk."

"Mostly." He started to straighten, then lost himself in the smell of her. "God, you feel good. What d'you wash this in?" He nuzzled her hair. "Smells like moonbeams."

"Really drunk," she said with a sigh. "Sit down. I'll get you some coffee."

"Don't want coffee. Doesn't sober you up, only wakes you up. And I'm awake, and I have something to say to you." He drew away then, and discovered he wasn't as steady as he'd hoped. "But I'll sit down." He did, heavily. "Hate getting drunk. Haven't done it like this since I played minor league. Did I tell you I played minor league ball? Triple A."

"No." Baffled, she stood her ground and watched him.

"Right out of high school. Two years. Thought I'd make it to the show. The majors. But I didn't, so I went to college, and now I write about people who did."

"I'm sorry."

"No." He waved that away. "I like writing. Always did. Like watching the games and seeing all the little dramas. If I'd've played, I'd be nearly washed up now. I'm almost thirty-three. Old man for the game." He focused on her, smiled. "You're the most beautiful woman I've ever seen in my life. You know, the kid looks just like you. Look at him, see you. It's spooky. I see you all the time. Minding my own business, and pop! There's your face in my head. What d'ya make of that?"

"I don't know." She wanted to be angry with him, really she did. But he was so foolishly drunk. "Why don't I take you upstairs, Coop? Put you to bed."

"I want you in my bed, Zoe. I want to make love with you. I want to touch you again."

She wanted that, too. Very much. But new lines had been drawn. "You said you wanted to talk to me."

"Do you know what your skin feels like? I can't describe it, it's all soft and smooth and warm. I started thinking about your skin when I was playing poker and getting drunk tonight. I won, too. Took a big pot with a pair of sixes. Pulled in over two hundred and fifty dollars."

"Congratulations."

"But I kept thinking about you. You have this little dimple right here." He nearly poked himself in the eye, then dragged a finger down his cheek to the corner of his mouth. "I kept thinking about that little dimple, and your skin, and those big eyes and killer legs. And I kept thinking how I like to watch you with the kid, like I do sometimes from upstairs, when you don't know. Didn't know that, did you?"

"No," she said quietly. "I didn't."

"Well, see…" He gestured wildly. "You've got this way of running your hand over his hair. It gets to me." He shook his head. "It really gets to me. Keenan loves me, you know. He told me he did. So did you."

"I know."

"And I meant everything I said this afternoon."

"I know." Sighing, she walked over to undo his shoelaces.

"Every word, Zoe. I've got my life set, just like I want it."

"Okay." She pried off his shoes, hefted his legs onto the couch.

"So you can stop popping into my head, 'cause it's not changing anything."

"I'll keep that in mind."

He was asleep before she bent over and kissed his cheek.

CHAPTER 10

As hangovers went, Coop knew, this would be a champ. He didn't have to open his eyes, he didn't have to move, not when his head was already beating like the Army drum corps.

He wasn't sure how he'd managed to get home and into bed, but the blur of the evening wasn't comforting. Still, he thought it best to wait to tax his brain.

Cautious, close to fearful, he opened his eyes. The little face directly above him had him jerking back, then moaning at the pain.

"Good morning," Keenan said cheerfully. "Did you sleep over?"

"I don't know." Coop lifted a hand to his head. "Where's your mother?"

"She's making my lunch. She said I could come in

and look at you if I didn't wake you up. I didn't wake you up, did I? I was really quiet."

"No." Coop closed his eyes again and prayed for oblivion.

"Are you sick? Do you have a tempature?" Keenan laid a small, light hand on Coop's aching forehead. "Mama can make it better. She always makes it better." Very gently, Keenan replaced his hand with a kiss. "Does that help?"

Oh, hell, Coop thought. Even a hangover didn't have a chance against this kid. "Yeah, thanks. What time is it?"

"The big hand's on the ten and the little hand's on the eight. You can sleep in my bed until you're better, and play with my toys."

"Thanks." Coop made the supreme effort and sat up. When his head rolled, he did his best to catch it in his hands. "Keenan, be a pal and ask your mom for some aspirin."

"Okay." He raced off, and the sound of his sneakers pounding the floor had Coop shuddering.

"Headache?" Zoe asked a moment later.

Coop lifted his head. She was still in her robe. The robe he remembered from the night before. He was beginning to remember quite a bit from the night before. "If you're going to yell at me, could you do it later?"

In answer, she held out aspirin and a glass filled with reddish liquid.

"What is it?"

"A remedy from Joe the bartender. He guarantees it'll take the edge off."

"Thanks."

There was a blast of a horn from outside that cut through Coop's skull like a dulled knife. While he was dealing with the shock of that, Keenan came racing back.

"Bye, Mama, bye!" He gave her a smacking kiss, then turned to hug Coop. "Bye."

As the door slammed behind him, Coop gulped down Joe's remedy.

"Do you want coffee?" Zoe ran her tongue around her teeth and tried not to smile. "Some breakfast?"

"You're not going to yell at me?"

"For barging in here, drunk, in the middle of the night? And for passing out on my sofa?" She paused just long enough to make her point. "No, I'm not going to yell at you. I figure you're suffering enough."

"I am, I promise you." He got up to follow her into the kitchen. "Not just physically. I feel like a total jerk."

"You *were* a total jerk." She poured a mug of coffee, set it on the table for him. "My mother's third husband had a fondness for bourbon. He swore eggs the morning after were the cure. How do you want them?"

"Scrambled would be good." He sat gingerly at the table. "I'm sorry, Zoe."

She kept her back to him. "For?"

"For being a jackass yesterday afternoon, and a bigger jackass last night."

"Oh, that." With the bacon frying, she chose a small bowl to scramble eggs in. "I don't imagine it's the first or the last time you'll be one."

"You didn't…" He shifted miserably. "Ah, you didn't tell Keenan I was…"

"Drunk and disorderly?" A half smile on her face, she glanced over her shoulder. "I told him you weren't feeling well and went to sleep on the couch. Which was close enough."

"Thanks. I wouldn't want him to think…you know. I don't make a habit out of it."

"So you said last night." She turned the bacon, whipped the eggs.

He watched her, gradually getting past the astonishment that she wasn't going to rub his nose in the mess he'd made of things. Remembering the afternoon before, when she'd stood up to him with all that pride and fury shining in her eyes. And the other night, when he'd fallen asleep on her couch—the way she'd looked when she slipped the boy from his arms into hers and carried him into bed.

A dozen other pictures, captured in so short a time,

flitted through his head, until they were whittled down
to one. This one. Zoe standing at the stove, with the
morning sun streaming over her tousled hair, her robe
flowing down, breakfast smells warming the room.

How could he have thought he didn't want this? Just
this. And what did he do now that he knew the truth?

"Food should help." She set the plate in front of him.
"I've got to get ready for work."

"Can you— Have you got a minute?"

"I suppose." She poured herself another cup of coffee. "I don't have to be in until ten."

He began to eat while thoughts scrambled in his
brain. "This is good. Thanks."

"You're welcome." She leaned back against the
counter. "Did you want something else?"

"Yeah." He ate more, hoping eggs equaled courage.
Then he put his fork down. It was the ninth inning,
he thought, and there were already two outs. "You. I
want you."

She smiled a little. "Coop, I doubt you're in any shape
for that, and I really have to go to work, so—"

"No, I don't mean that. I mean I do, but not—" He
broke off, took a long, deep breath. "I want you to
marry me."

"I beg your pardon?"

"I think you should marry me. It's a good idea."
Somewhere in the back of his mind, he realized, he'd

been working on this all along. He had it figured. "You can quit your night job and go back to school if you want. Or open that flower shop. Whatever. I think that's what we should do."

"Really." Because her hand was unsteady, she set her coffee down. "Well that's very generous of you, Coop, but I don't have to get married to do any of those things. So thanks just the same."

He stared. "No? You're saying no? But you love me. You said it. Twice you said it."

"We can make it three," she said evenly. "Yes, I love you. No, I won't marry you. Now I really have to get ready for work."

"Just a damn minute." Hangover forgotten, he pushed back from the table and rose. "What kind of game is this? You love me, your kid's crazy about me, we're terrific in bed, I even know how to drive a damn car pool, but you won't marry me."

"You're such an idiot. You're such a fool. Do you think because I didn't put up a struggle before I fell into your bed that you can have everything your own way? When you want it, how you want it? Well, you're wrong. And you *are* a jackass."

He winced as she stormed from the room. Strike one, he thought. And he hadn't even seen the pitch.

But the game wasn't over, he thought grimly, until the fat lady sang.

* * *

Zoe was still steaming when she came home from work. Of all the arrogant, interfering, self-absorbed idiots she'd ever known, J. Cooper McKinnon took the gold medal. Imagine him telling her that marrying him was a good idea, then ticking off all the advantages she'd gain.

Oh, he thought he was a prize.

One day he's telling her to get any ideas of sneaking him into a relationship out of her head. As if she'd been baiting traps for him. The next he's taking pity on her and offering her a big male helping hand.

She should have bitten it off.

Not once, not once had he said what she would bring to him, what he felt for her, what he wanted. Not once had he brought up the fact that he could or would accept another man's child as his own.

She jerked open the front door, slammed it. He could take his half-baked proposal and sit on it.

"Mama! Hey, Mama!" Keenan zipped into the living room and grabbed her hand. "Come on, come on. We've got a surprise."

"What surprise? What are you doing home, Keenan? You're supposed to be at the Finklemans'."

"Coop's here." He tugged manfully on her hand. "We have a surprise. And we have a secret. And you have to come *now!*"

"All right, I'm coming." She braced herself and let Keenan drag her into the kitchen.

There were flowers, banks of them, vases and baskets overflowing on the counters, on the floor, on the windowsills. There was music, some soft, dreamy classical sonata, on the radio. The table was set, crystal she'd never seen before glinting in the sunlight, a bottle of champagne chilling in a silver bucket. And Coop was standing there, in a neatly pressed shirt and slacks.

"It's a surprise," Keenan announced gleefully. "We made everything look nice so you'd like it. And Mrs. Finkleman said we could use the glasses and the plates. And Mr. Finkleman made his special chicken 'cause it's resistible."

"Irresistible," Coop said, his eyes on Zoe. "You, ah, said you didn't need flowers and candlelight, but I've never taken you out on a date. I thought this was the next-best thing."

"Do you like it, Mama? Do you?"

"Yes, it's very nice." She bent down to kiss Keenan. "Thank you."

"I get to go to the Finklemans' so you can have romance."

"Ah, come on, kid." Coop scooped Keenan up. "Let's get you started. You were supposed to keep quiet about it," he muttered when he carried the boy outside.

"What's romance?"

"I'll tell you later."

Satisfied with that, Keenan draped his arm around Coop's neck. "Are you gonna tell Mama the secret about us all getting married?"

"That's the plan."

"And you'll live with us and you can be my Daddy and that'll be okay?"

"That'll be great. It'll be perfect." He stopped by the fence to press a kiss to Keenan's mouth. "I love you, Keenan."

"Okay." He squeezed his arms hard around Coop's neck. "Bye."

"Bye."

"Yoo-hoo!" Mrs. Finkleman stood at the back door. She sent Coop a wink and an exaggerated thumbs-up sign before whisking Keenan inside.

She was standing pretty much where Coop had left her when he came back. He wasn't sure whether or not that was a good sign.

"So, ready for some champagne?"

"Coop, this is very nice of you, but—"

"Like the flowers?" Nervous as a cat, he popped the cork.

"Yes, they're wonderful, but—"

"I couldn't get them where you work, or I'd have spoiled the surprise. Keenan really gave me a hand setting things up." He handed her the glass, and when she was distracted, he leaned in for a slow, warm kiss. "Hi."

"Coop." She had to wait for her heart to finish its lazy somersault. "I know you must have gone to a lot of trouble—"

"I should have gone to it before. I didn't know I wanted to."

"Oh, Lord." She turned away and struggled to get her emotions under control. "I've given you the wrong impression this time. I don't need the trappings. I don't have to have romantic evenings and—" she waved toward the tapers on the table, waiting to be lit "—candlelight."

"Sure you do. So do I, when they're with you."

"You're trying to charm me," she said unsteadily. "That's new."

"You know what I am. The way this house is set up, we've practically been living together for the past month or so. People get to know each other quicker that way than just by socializing. So you know what I am, and you fell for me anyway."

She took a drink. "You're awfully smug about it. I told you my feelings are my responsibility, and that holds true. A romantic dinner doesn't change it."

It looked like strike two, but Coop knew that if he was going to go down, he'd go down swinging. "So I want to give you a nice evening. Is something wrong with that? I want to do better than propose over scrambled eggs when I've got a hangover." His voice had risen, and he bit down on it. "Damn it, this is my first time, have a little tolerance. No, don't say anything, let me finish this. You don't need me." He took another long breath. "Not for taking care of things, for you or the kid, I mean, for mowing the grass or putting stupid barbecue grills together. What about what I need, Zoe?"

She blinked at him. "Well, that's just it. Don't you see? You made it clear that you don't need or want ties. I come with ties, Coop."

"I made it clear," he muttered. "I didn't make anything clear, because I didn't know. Didn't want to know. I was scared. There. You feel better knowing that?" He glared at her. "I was scared, because I need you. Because I need to see your face and hear your voice and smell your hair. I just need you to be there. And I need to help you mow the grass and put the grill together. I need you to need me back."

"Oh." She shut her eyes. "I like hearing that."

"Then tell me you will." He took her arms until she opened her eyes again. "It's my last swing, Zoe. Marry me."

"I—" Yes. She wanted to say yes. "It's not just me, Coop."

"You think I don't want the kid? God, open your eyes. I'm crazy about him. I fell for him before I fell for you. I want to marry both of you, then maybe have another kid or two so I can start out on the ground floor. We already worked that out."

"You— Who did what?"

He swore, stepped back, shrugged. "I kind of ran it by the kid. I figured I should smooth the way a little, and find out where he stood." When she just stared, he jammed his hands in his pockets. "It didn't seem fair not to bring him into it, since he'd be mine."

"Yours," she murmured, staring blindly into her wine.

"Since you two are a team, it would be sort of like an expansion. Anyway, he's for it. So it's two against one."

"I see."

"Maybe I don't know a lot about the daddy stuff, but I love him. That's a good start."

She looked at him again, looked into his eyes. Her heart opened, flooded. "It's a good one, all right."

"I love you." His hands relaxed in his pockets. "That's the first time I've said that to any woman—except my mother. I love you, Zoe. So why don't you marry me and give me and the kid a break?"

"It looks like I'm outvoted." She lifted a hand to his cheek.

"Is that a yes?"

"That's definitely a yes." She laughed as he swung her into his arms. "Daddy."

"I like the sound of that." He crushed his lips down on hers. "I like it a lot."

* * * * *